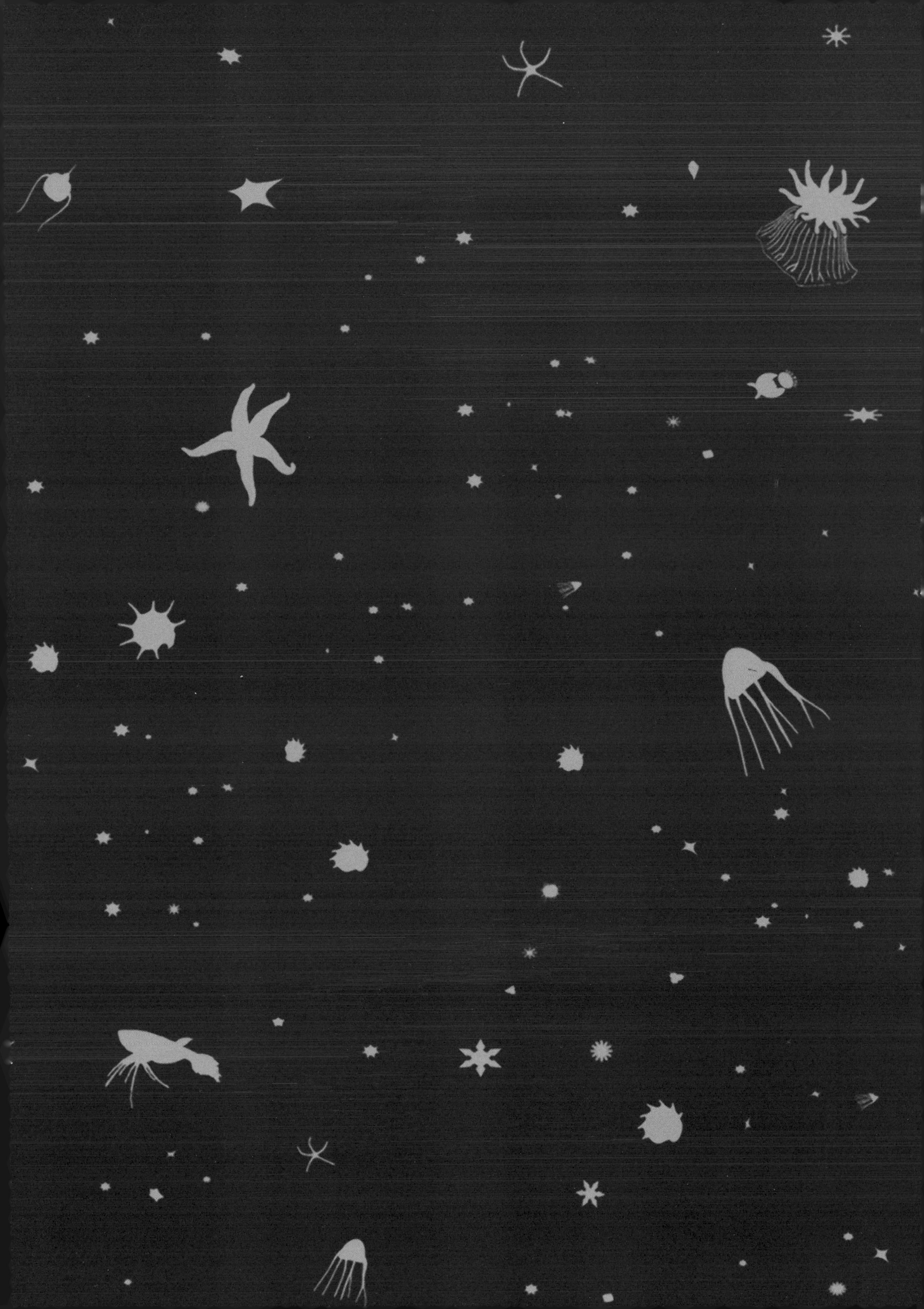

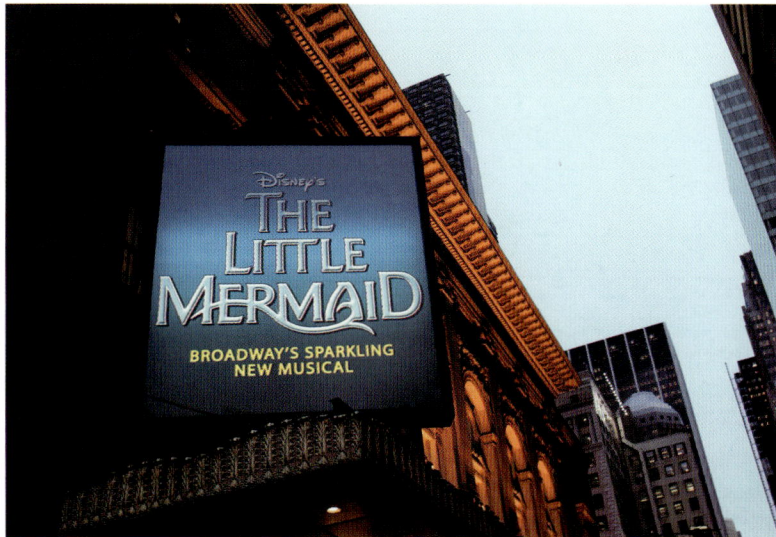

This book is dedicated to
the memory of
HOWARD ASHMAN
(1950–1991)

And to little mermaids . . . everywhere.

I'll tell you a tale

of the bottomless blue

Sierra Boggess and J.J. Singleton

Norm Lewis and Sierra Boggess

Sierra Boggess, Sherie Rene Scott, and Tyler Maynard

DISNEY's THE LITTLE MERMAID

A BROADWAY MUSICAL

From the Deep Blue Sea to the Great White Way

Written by Michael Lassell

A Welcome Book

DISNEY
EDITIONS
NEW YORK

PRECEDING PAGES: Sierra Boggess
ABOVE: Sherie Rene Scott

Disney Theatrical Productions
under the direction of
Thomas Schumacher
presents

Disney's **THE LITTLE MERMAID**

Music
ALAN MENKEN

Lyrics
HOWARD ASHMAN & GLENN SLATER

Book
DOUG WRIGHT

Based on the Hans Christian Andersen story
and the Disney film written and directed by John Musker & Ron Clements

Starring

SIERRA BOGGESS   SEAN PALMER

NORM LEWIS   TITUSS BURGESS   EDDIE KORBICH   JONATHAN FREEMAN

DERRICK BASKIN   TYLER MAYNARD   TREVOR BRAUN   BRIAN D'ADDARIO   CODY HANFORD   J.J. SINGLETON

and

SHERIE RENE SCOTT

ADRIAN BAILEY   CATHRYN BASILE   HEIDI BLICKENSTAFF   JAMES BROWN III   ROBERT CREIGHTON
CICILY DANIELS   JOHN TREACY EGAN   TIM FEDERLE   MERWIN FOARD   BEN HARTLEY
MEREDITH INGLESBY   MICHELLE LOOKADOO   JOANNE MANNING   ALAN MINGO, JR.   ZAKIYA YOUNG MIZEN
BETSY MORGAN   ARBENDER J. ROBINSON   BAHIYAH SAYYED GAINES   BRET SHUFORD   JASON SNOW
CHELSEA MORGAN STOCK   KAY TRINIDAD   PRICE WALDMAN   DANIEL J. WATTS

Scenic Design
GEORGE TSYPIN

Costume Design
TATIANA NOGINOVA

Lighting Design
NATASHA KATZ

Sound Design
JOHN SHIVERS

Hair Design
DAVID BRIAN BROWN

Makeup Design
ANGELINA AVALLONE

Projection & Video Design
SVEN ORTEL

Dance Arrangements
DAVID CHASE

Music Coordinator
MICHAEL KELLER

Fight Director
RICK SORDELET

Casting
TARA RUBIN CASTING

Associate Producer
TODD LACY

Associate Director
BRIAN HILL

Associate Choreographer
TARA YOUNG

Technical Director
DAVID BENKEN

Production Supervisor
CLIFFORD SCHWARTZ

Press Representative
BONEAU / BRYAN-BROWN

Orchestrations by
DANNY TROOB

Music Director
Incidental Music & Vocal Arrangements by
MICHAEL KOSARIN

Choreography by
STEPHEN MEAR

Directed by
FRANCESCA ZAMBELLO

contents

from

the producer

TWENTY YEARS AGO I ARRIVED at Walt Disney Feature Animation as a first-time staff producer and was immediately faced with a strange new world of techniques, form, and process that I knew nothing about. Growing up in the theater and far away from the world of film, I was clearly a stranger in a strange new land.

That first week my dear friend (and all-too-unsung hero of the second generation of Disney Animation), Peter Schneider, took me to a rough screening of a new film that was still in process and would mark Disney's return to classic fairy tales. Ironically, back then the idea of animation, let alone a beautifully animated musical fairy tale, was considered such a major risk that the animators were relegated to working in an inexpensive warehouse space several miles from the studio Walt Disney had built fifty years earlier.

Needless to say, the film we were screening that day was *The Little Mermaid*. It was based on the Hans Christian Andersen tale, but reimagined by the extraordinarily talented writing, directing, and producing team of John Musker and Ron Clements—without whom the notion of an "animation renaissance" would be impossible to contemplate.

What made that day's screening come to life, even in basic black and white, was the song score by Alan Menken and Howard Ashman. This was theater music made completely new by its marriage to animation. A new era was beginning, and I felt immediately at home—even as a mere observer.

Those memorable songs not only brought to life the story of a young mermaid who dreamt of a world beyond the sea, but they also launched Disney's artistic and financial return to the top of the animation heap.

Tragically, the brilliant Howard Ashman died before their equally famous collaborations of *Beauty and the Beast* and *Aladdin* were released. Even so, Alan Menken continues adding to one of the most astounding songwriting catalogs of all time.

Over the twenty years I have known Alan, through countless screenings, rehearsals, recording sessions, story pitches, workshops, and readings, I have never stopped being amazed or delighted at his talent and range.

"If music be the food of love . . ." Alan is perhaps America's greatest Iron Chef.

The Little Mermaid's reincarnation for the stage is a tribute to all of the people who created it. Our glorious director Francesca Zambello, choreographer Stephen Mear, Alan and his writing partners Howard Ashman and Glenn Slater, brilliant book writer Doug Wright, and designers George Tsypin, Tanya Noginova, and Natasha Katz well deserve the nightly standing ovation they share with the rest of the creative team and the celebrated original Broadway cast illustrated on these pages.

—THOMAS SCHUMACHER

OPPOSITE: Ariel gets her first glimpse of Prince Eric in Act I of Broadway's *The Little Mermaid*.

rock music, children's theater, and underground hip culture. Disney empowered him, as executive producer of the film, to strongly influence every aspect of the script, character concepts, and, of course, songs and score. With the great team of John Musker and Ron Clements writing and directing, we went through a process of story work, song demos, storyboards, character-voice recording, animation, and finally the recording of our songs and my underscore with what then seemed to me to be an enormous number of musicians and singers. As much as we might have hoped for some recognition for our little animated project, nothing could have prepared us for the reaction that greeted our *Mermaid*. We had deliberately not cast big-name talent, favoring actors and singers from the world of theater: Jodi Benson, Sam Wright, Pat Carroll, etc. We had resisted any attempt to put the agenda of creating a hit song ahead of what was needed dramatically. People loved it!

The fairy tale aspect of our lives at Disney was to soon undergo a dark transformation, when Howard succumbed to the ravages of AIDS midway into the creation of *Beauty and the Beast* and *Aladdin*. His carefully guarded secret was revealed to me on the night of the Academy Awards in 1990, when between us, we won three Oscars for *The Little Mermaid*. His health gave way and within a year, he was gone; but not before we had completed the songs to *Beauty* and what we thought was the complete score to *Aladdin*.

MY JOURNEY WITH *THE LITTLE MERMAID* began in 1986, when Howard Ashman called me about collaborating with him on songs for an animated musical based on the Hans Christian Andersen fairy tale. Our last work together had been our monster, Off-Broadway hit, *Little Shop of Horrors*. Since then, we'd been working with different partners; Howard with Marvin Hamlisch, on *Smile*, and me with Tom Eyen, on *Kicks*. The excitement about Howard and me reteaming was, at first, the prime consideration on my mind. From *God Bless You, Mr. Rosewater* to *Little Shop*, we had found a voice of our own, both as songwriters and musical theater dramatists. The advantage of working with a lyricist who was also a book writer and a director was huge for me. Now we would get to apply that voice in service to an art form we had both grown up with and loved, plus, with my year-old daughter, I had been rediscovering all of the old Disney classics through the miracle of home video. I'd sit on the couch, with her and lose myself in the magic of *Cinderella* or *Pinocchio* or *Snow White* or *Peter Pan*, among so many other great classic titles.

Our assignment was to create a new classic that could sit on the shelf alongside the others. In Howard Ashman, Disney had found the perfect artist to accomplish this. He comfortably straddled the worlds of traditional musical theater, cutting-edge

from

Following Howard's passing, when it was decided to make major changes in the story of *Aladdin*, Tim Rice stepped in to help me complete the song score. Years later, when *Beauty* was adapted for Broadway, Tim again collaborated with me on the new songs.

Years went by, with many new animated projects (*Pocahontas, The Hunchback of Notre Dame, Hercules, Home on the Range*) and collaborators (Stephen Schwartz, David Zippel, Glenn Slater). I had the experience of coming back full circle to the New York stage with *Beauty and the Beast* and Madison Square Garden's *A Christmas Carol*. *The Little Mermaid* was the precious gem that had started this miracle, but other projects were following in its wake and achieving much greater success at the box office—*The Lion King*, in particular. It seemed that *Mermaid* could not be brought to the stage because of the need to spend over half of the evening under the sea and where *Beauty* seemed practically written for the stage, *Mermaid* felt much more limited to its conception as an animated film.

Then came the day when Tom Schumacher brought up the topic of developing our baby for Broadway. Would I commence the process of expanding the story and score for the stage, in hopes that a more avant-garde approach might help solve the physical staging challenges? Yes! I chose as my lyricist a brilliant young man, Glenn Slater, who had worked with me on the animated musical, *Home on the Range*, among lots of other projects that fell away in development. Much of the score that now is heard nightly at the Lunt-Fontanne was written in that early stage, but nothing could move forward

without the right concept of how to stage the show. Finally, with the inclusion of Francesca Zambello and the wonderful and fearless team of designers who worked with her in the world of opera, this musical became a real possibility. Along with Doug Wright, we immersed ourselves in the process of shaping an evening in the theater that would both expand on and preserve the magic of our original creation.

Ariel's ballad, "Part of Your World," now had a real counterbalancing moment for Prince Eric's "Her Voice." A new production number, featuring Flounder and Ariel's sisters, "She's in Love," joined Sebastian's "Under the Sea" in bringing the house down. In total we added twelve new song moments to the original seven. The look, the sound, and the story had evolved, and yet it still works its magic with audiences, both young and old. I think much of the reason for that is Glenn Slater's and my commitment to seamlessly integrating our new material into the old. Above all else, Howard Ashman's heart and voice would be kept alive and vibrant, and every night at the Lunt I feel him come alive again, as he would whenever Mrs. Potts sang "Beauty and the Beast" or Lumiere sang "Be Our Guest" from that same stage. The journey continues, for me, for Disney, and for the entire world.

—ALAN MENKEN

OPPOSITE: Ariel, the little mermaid, from the 1989 Disney film.

the composer

19

ARIEL'S STORY

part one

OPPOSITE: A costume sketch by Tatiana Noginova for
The Little Mermaid's Broadway debut.

WELCOME TO THE MANY WORLDS of Ariel, the Little Mermaid, a princess whose realm is both under the briny blue sea—where she grew up as the youngest daughter of King Triton, mythic ruler of the oceans of the world—and on the golden land, in the kingdom of Prince Eric, the worthy human she comes to love. Our book celebrates the Disney stage musical version of the yarn, which opened on Broadway in January of 2008, but the story of a little mermaid who sells her voice for legs in order to live and love on shore is one of the most popular and enduring fairy tales of all time, and it has inspired poets, painters, playwrights, composers, and dancers for over 170 years. Wherever she appears, *The Little Mermaid* captivates people's hearts, so it's not surprising that her story should have found its way into a Disney animated film and now into live theater.

The character we now know as Ariel began her life in Denmark in the first half of the nineteenth century, and she has become something of an icon of that European nation, representing the spirit of the country and its people. In fact, if you happen to find yourself in Copenhagen, the country's capital, the chances are you will take time to visit a diminutive sculpture that sits in the harbor alongside what is now called Churchill Park. There, perched on a rock, is the figure of a mermaid—surprisingly small and close to shore—looking wistfully out to sea.

The statue, with its legs and fins artfully ambiguous, was sculpted by Edward Eriksen and drew its inspiration from the classical dancer Ellen Price in Fini Henriques's ballet, *The Little Mermaid*, which was based on the story published by Hans Christian Andersen in 1836. Local brewer Carl Jacobsen—

son of the creator of Carlsberg beer—was so moved by Price's 1909 performance that he asked her to pose for a sculpture that would be his gift to the city. (At first, she agreed, but when she found out how little clothing the figure would be wearing, and how public an area it would inhabit, the modest danseuse declined the honor, and the sculptor's wife modeled instead.)

The Little Mermaid, or *Den lille havfrue*, as she is known in Danish, has sat faithfully on her rock come rain or shine, snow or fog, since August 23, 1913, through two world wars and more than a few assaults on her dignity by vandals (she's had her head cut off and replaced twice). And although most of the world knows very little of Ellen Price and Carl Jacobsen, almost everyone knows Hans Christian Andersen, whose stories read at bedtime have sent millions of children to sweet dreams.

Like many of the most potent fairy tales, *The Little Mermaid* serves the function of the myths of ancient cultures. She speaks to something inherently human—no matter how many times her tale is retold or in what medium or what alterations are made to the original Andersen text. Her story—she is the quintessential outsider with her heart set on belonging to a world outside her own—moves us, because she is part of something almost every one of us has felt at some time in our lives.

OPPOSITE: The famous statue of The Little Mermaid in Copenhagen, Denmark.
ABOVE: Danish author Hans Christian Andersen.

The millions of Danes and foreign tourists who visit the statue of the little mermaid today are evidence of the enormous affection in which Andersen is held, both in his native country and all over the world. The writer himself—born into poverty, poorly educated, ungainly, unattractive, unpopular, and deeply conflicted about his own role in the adult world of romance—would no doubt be astounded how universal his stories have become. Happily, he came to know the fame, respect, and financial success he so longed for as a child. When asked why he had never written an autobiography, he replied that he had, and he'd called it *The Ugly Duckling*—although it's doubtful that Andersen ever fully believed in his own transformation into the beautiful swan at the end of that tale.

The book you hold in your hand is the story of Ariel and her journey from the pages of Andersen's 1836 book to the Great White Way 172 years later. Like the statue of *The Little Mermaid* in Copenhagen, the book is an expression of affec-

tion for the author himself and his stories—not only *The Little Mermaid*, but also *The Ugly Duckling*, *The Princess and the Pea*, *The Red Shoes*, *The Brave Tin Soldiers*, *Thumbelina*, *The Little Match Girl*, *The Emperor's New Clothes*, and so many others. It is also a tribute to one of Andersen's central themes: the transcendent, healing power of love. Her longing for love is what motivates Ariel; her discovery of true love is what saves and frees her in the end.

In the Hans Christian Andersen version of the story, the little mermaid, who is only ten years old at the beginning of the story, longs for the immortal soul she will gain if she can find true love with a human in the world above. Andersen did not invent mermaids, of course. Legends of merfolk had been floating around for generations, like rumors of Atlantis. Sailors returning from their voyages offered up fantastical accounts of ocean beings that are human from the middle up but sport fins, scales, and tails from the waist down. Frequently, the highly imaginative and emotional fables involved beautiful young maidens who lured men to a watery grave with their ethereal voices.

It was Andersen's unique contribution to mermaid lore to see the story not from the perspective of a sailor destroyed by a cold-hearted monster in beautiful form (a deep-sea wolf in

LEFT: Hans Christian Andersen imagined by Anne Grahame Johnstone.
ABOVE: An 1890 illustration by E.S. Hardy.

ABOVE: Disney development art for
The Little Mermaid film.

sheep's clothing). Instead, "the Danish Dickens"—who always considered himself a misfit—saw the tale from the mermaid's point of view. The nameless mermaid of his imagination was pure, virtuous, and good. There is little doubt that Andersen considered true love to be a kind of salvation, and he spent his own life looking for it without success. (One of the unavailable objects of his misguided affection was the internationally renowned opera singer Jenny Lind—known as "the Swedish Nightingale"—who had no romantic feelings for the hapless writer whatsoever.)

For many generations, Andersen's story inspired other artistic individuals, and most of the great illustrators of the world have devoted their energies to depicting the story for one elaborately printed edition of the book after another (even Andersen did drawings of his story). In 1989, the world had its first chance to see the Disney animated film version of *The Little Mermaid* (although Walt Disney himself had considered a film version as early as 1940). The feature animated film, with music by Alan Menken and songs by Menken and the late Howard Ashman, instantly became part of Disney's leg-

endary legacy, and its young heroine became one of the studio's all-time favorite characters. Both a box-office and critical hit, the film catapulted Disney animation out of the doldrums that had set in after Walt's death in 1966 and changed the medium forever. Its score and one of its two nominated songs ("Under the Sea") won Academy Awards.

The film instantly entered the collective database of popular culture and left in its magic wake an entire generation of children, especially girls, who both admire and adore the adventurous adolescent Ariel (a "teener of the sea"). Actually, the mermaid has no name at all in the Andersen original. And although the name Ariel appears in both the Bible (as an angel) and in the works of William Shakespeare (as a spirit), it was Disney's *The Little Mermaid* that made it the popular girl's name it is today.

The film's plot was considerably updated, too, to the world of today. Animated Ariel is more of a recognizable contemporary adolescent than a mythical denizen of the deep. She has a much sunnier and much more modern disposition. She can be as fiery as her flowing red hair when she wants to be and as courageous in the face of danger as she is kind to her friends and devoted in her affection for the prince.

Disney's animated *The Little Mermaid* opened on November 15, 1989, starring Broadway ingenue Jodi Benson as the voice of Ariel and featuring an eclectic score. The tunes ranged from the aspirational ballad, "Part of Your World," to the romantic "Kiss the Girl," and the instantly popular calypso-inspired "Under the Sea" (appropriately, the name of this up-tempo West Indian beat—calypso—derives from the sea nymph who detained Odysseus for seven years in Homer's *The Odyssey*).

The Little Mermaid took the public by surprise. In Chicago, Roger Ebert wrote, "Here at last, once again, is the kind of liberating, original, joyful Disney animation that we all remember from *Snow White*, *Pinocchio*, and the other first-generation classics."

And writing for *The New York Times*, Janet Maslin found *The Little Mermaid* to be "a marvel of skillful animation" with "witty songwriting and smart planning." Further, she found: "It is designed to delight filmgoers of every conceivable stripe. Teenagers will appreciate the story's rebellious heroine, a spunky, flirty little nymph who defies her father's wishes when she leaves his underwater kingdom to explore the world above the ocean's surface. Adults will be charmed by the film's bright, outstandingly pretty look and by its robust score. Small children will be enchanted by the film's sunniness and by its perfect simplicity."

OPPOSITE: Ariel with her two best friends, Sebastian and Flounder, both of whom were Disney additions to the original story.

The film ranked in the top ten highest-grossing films of the year. Ariel, the first new member of the Disney inner family to come along in decades, found an instant fan base, particularly among young girls. Indeed, the demand for merchandise related to the film was so great, Leonard Maltin notes in his book, *The Disney Films*, that the studio's merchandising department was ill prepared to meet it.

What surprised reviewers and delighted audiences was the giant leap forward in the art of animation the film represented. Disney's cartoon features had always favored music, and the Disney songbook is long and deep with Academy Award–winning tunes, the first of which was "When You Wish Upon a Star" from *Pinocchio* in 1940. But *The Little Mermaid*, its audience realized from the beginning, was not only the first Disney film since *Sleeping Beauty* in 1959 to be based on a classic fairy tale, it was also the first full-scale animated film musical (a somewhat different-colored sea horse altogether from a film that has music in it): *Snow White and the Seven Dwarfs* is a movie with songs; *The Little Mermaid* movie is a full-scale, Broadway-style musical—on film.

It was Disney animator Ron Clements who happened on Hans Christian Andersen's "The Little Mermaid" in a Los Angeles bookstore in the mid-1980s. Clements, who had worked on *The Rescuers* and *Pete's Dragon*, had also served as supervising animator on *The Fox and the Hound*, and had directed *The Great Mouse Detective*, instantly saw the way to apply his studio's particular magic to Andersen's story. While some of the original would have to be altered to make the story palatable for a modern audience consisting largely of children, Clements believed he could make it work. In Andersen's story, although the mermaid got legs, walking on them caused her so much pain that she felt as if she were walking on knives. The prince in Andersen's story does not fall in love with her at all. He marries someone else, and the ending is far from happily ever after.

Clements brought his Little Mermaid idea to the weekly Gong Show, and it was summarily gonged because Disney's live-action division was preparing a sequel to the 1984 Tom Hanks/Daryl Hannah film *Splash*, and executives thought that two films in development about mermaids at the same time was one too many. But the powers that be couldn't get the idea of an animated Little Mermaid out of their collective creative mind: The project was un-gonged, and Ron Clements was given a green light to explore the possibility of a feature animated film based on Andersen's story.

Given the go-ahead, Clements, a graduate of the animation department at California Institute of the Arts, which was founded by Walt Disney, brought in John Musker, his partner on several films. Musker's credits included animation on *The Fox and the Hound* and *The Great Mouse Detective*, which he also directed. Clements and Musker, Leonard Maltin wrote, "were lucky enough to join the studio at a time when they could learn from some of the remaining 'old masters,' but they were young enough to have ideas of their own that they were eager to implement." The two would go on to be creative heroes of the Disney animation cycle that followed *The Little Mermaid*.

Now, it happens that by the mid-1980s, Disney animation was not the trailblazing art form Walt Disney had created. Computers were taking over the work of animators, and the high cost of the medium—compared to flagging box-office interest—had already sparked some talk of the studio giving up on animation altogether. This was a possibility that Roy E. Disney, Walt's nephew and the son of the studio's cofounder, Roy O. Disney, found untenable. Roy E. Disney was committed to the studio continuing to succeed in feature animation. In 1984, the corporation hired Michael Eisner as its new CEO. Eisner brought Jeffrey Katzenberg with him from Paramount as head of film production; Roy E. Disney himself became the head of animation.

Part of the energy the new regime brought to the Burbank, California, lot were weekly meetings the staff called "Gong Shows," after Chuck Barris's absurdist TV talent show. The animators would pitch possible film ideas and almost invariably the ideas would be "gonged" (shot down by Disney, Katzenberg, or Eisner).

ABOVE: Walt's nephew, Roy E. Disney, was a champion of animation at the Studio.
RIGHT: John Musker (left) and Ron Clements wrote and directed the 1989 *Little Mermaid* film.

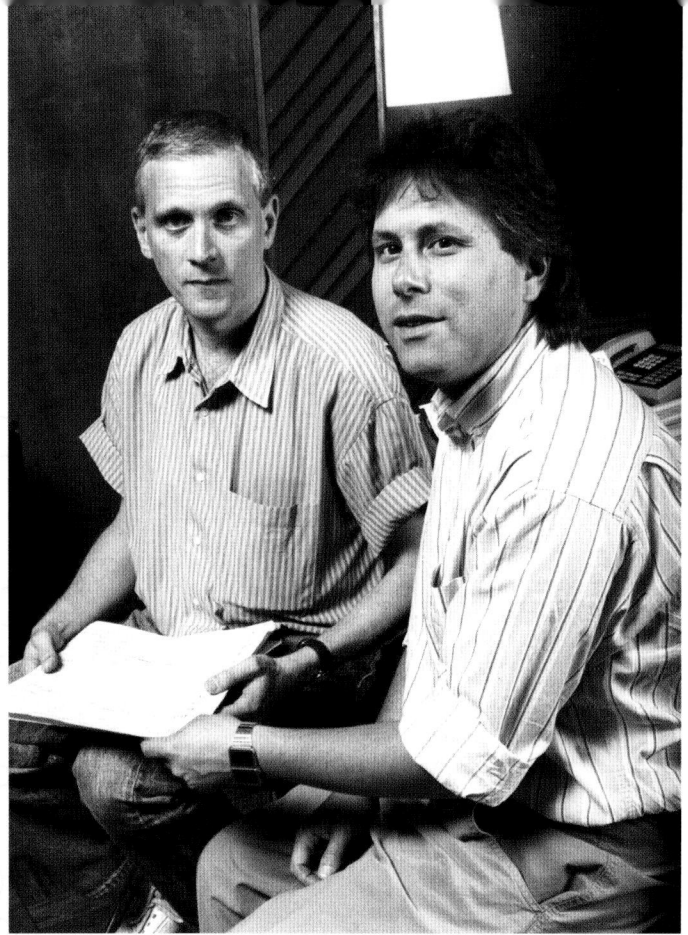

The real credit for the musical structure of *The Little
Mermaid* (and for the Broadway-izing of the animation
landscape) goes to a pair of transplanted New York theater
professionals. In one of those unpredictable turns of fate,
Disney engaged Baltimore-born director, producer, playwright,
and lyricist Howard Ashman to coproduce the film.

Ashman, a popular and well-known off-Broadway theater
force, had gone to Hollywood to scout for a new project after
the disappointing failure of *Smile*, a Broadway show he wrote
and directed, with music by Marvin Hamlisch; it played at the
Lunt-Fontanne Theatre—for forty-eight performances. Ashman
was nominated for a Tony Award for Best Book, but he had
grown disenchanted with the New York theater. On the West
Coast, Ashman was offered many live-action films but chose
The Little Mermaid. He invited composer Alan Menken to join
him.

Ashman and Menken had met at the legendary BMI
Lehman Engel Musical Theater Workshop in New York City
in the late '70s. Menken's first produced show, in 1978,
was *God Bless You, Mr. Rosewater*, an adaptation of a Kurt
Vonnegut novel, at the off-off-Broadway WPA Theater, where
Ashman was creative director. In 1982, Ashman and Menken
teamed up on a little show called *The Little Shop of Horrors*,
cementing their reputations.

Originally surprised that Ashman wanted to work for
Disney, Menken agreed. "I said yes because I wanted to
work with Howard again," remembers the composer, who
had never written a film score. "But Howard convinced me
that animation was one of the last bastions of musical theater."
As for his own interest, Ashman said at the time, "I grew up
on *Pinocchio* and *Peter Pan*, and the idea of creating something that could live comfortably on the shelf with those films
struck me as something difficult but wonderful to attempt."

As a co-producer on the animated *Little Mermaid*,
Ashman was involved in every aspect of the making of the
film, including the script by Clements and Musker. Ashman,
says Menken, "had a strong concept for the music, as well
as for the lyrics. He would come in not only with the words,
but the whole dramatic thrust and style of the song, and how
we were going to use the underscore." Ashman was bringing
his expertise in the musical theater to musical film: "In almost
every musical ever written," Ashman explained, drawing on
the lessons learned at the Lehman Engel workshop, "there's a
place, usually early in the show, where the leading lady sits
down on something—in *Brigadoon* it's a tree stump; in *Little
Shop of Horrors* it's a trash can—and sings about what she
wants most in life. We borrowed this classic rule of Broadway
musical construction for 'Part of Your World.'"

"When they played 'Part of Your World' in the board-
room, *Mermaid* was in production," remembers Disney animation executive Peter Schneider, himself an émigré from the
world of theater, and "everyone went, 'I want to work on that
movie!' Because it was so joyous." In fact, the whole animation team was excited by the process of creating *Mermaid*
(which would later be the case with the Broadway production,
too).

Disney's First Little Mermaid

DANISH ARTIST KAY NIELSEN (whose first name rhymes with *high*) had the kind of childhood Hans Christian Andersen could only have dreamed of. Nielsen was born in 1886; his mother was a celebrated actress, his father the director of the Royal Theater in Copenhagen. At eighteen he went to study art in Paris and returned a decade later to a career as an actor and stage designer. He subsequently became world-renowned for his art nouveau illustrations of fairy tales, including a 1924 edition of Hans Christian Andersen. In 1936, legendary stage director Max Reinhardt brought Nielsen to the United States to design a production of *Everyman* at the Hollywood Bowl.

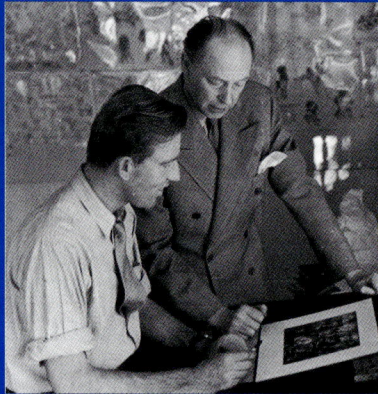

ABOVE: Artist Kay Nielsen (standing) with Bill Wallett.

The production impressed Walt Disney enough that he convinced Nielsen to work at the Studio as a sketch artist, story man, and designer. Nielsen's only significant work to wind up on film, however, was for the "Night on Bald Mountain" sequence of *Fantasia* in 1940 (for which he was one of four men credited as art director). Among Nielsen's other projects was a series of storyboards in pastel for a short animated version of *The Little Mermaid* that was never made. The drawings survived, though, and so inspired the makers of the 1989 *Little Mermaid* that they, too, gave Nielsen screen credit—for "visual development."

As completed, there is very little about *The Little Mermaid* film that didn't owe a good measure of its creative origin to Broadway musical tradition. Ashman, who is credited as the energetic genius behind the film by Schneider, even brought in Broadway performers to do the voices: Pat Carroll (as the seawitch Ursula), Rene Auberjonois (as Louie the French chef), and, as Ariel, one Jodi Benson, who just happened to have sung the leading role in Ashman's poor unfortunate *Smile*.

It wasn't until the creative team was well into its work on *The Little Mermaid* film that they discovered Walt Disney himself had considered a film version of the tale in the early 1940s. Disney had at that time asked Danish illustrator Kay Nielsen (who had been hired to create the forbidding visual world of *Fantasia*'s "Night on Bald Mountain" sequence) to do a rough storyboard for a short Little Mermaid film, which the talented Mr. Nielsen did. Those drawings, quite dark, as is the Andersen tale, and quite abstract, never convinced Walt Disney to make a Little Mermaid, but the groundwork—and the studio's history with the property—was invaluable to those working on the film more than forty years later.

Unusual for a major studio film, the core creative figures were all working beyond and outside their previous experience, but the collaboration somehow created the right atmosphere for success, and there was real excitement in the animation building while the film was in the works. "Sometimes that's part of the journey," says Schneider. "You start with people who are unsure, and you have great faith in them. You believe in them, and maybe they'll make magic." For Schneider, it was the combination of Ashman's high panache—and his naivete as an outsider to the world of animation—and the more conservative but accomplished talents of Musker and Clements that made the film come together.

"Everyone deserves credit for this film," says Schneider, "but Howard was a story genius. He had sworn he would never work on Broadway again, and in some fabulous way he found a home at Disney Animation because it was everything he was looking for: a cocoon, a creative bunch of people. It was small, it was intimate, it was hands on." The team of Clements, Musker, Ashman, and Menken put every aspect of the original Andersen story under the microscope, kept what they could, and changed everything else.

TOP: The actors behind *The Little Mermaid*'s film voices.
LEFT: Animation executive Peter Schneider with Musker and Clements.
OPPOSITE: Ursula, the big blue sea witch.

Not only did the team christen the story's young heroine, they gave her a circle of friends, too: Sebastian the Jamaican crab, Scuttle the addlepated seagull, and timid but faithful little Flounder. Even Ursula the bluish seawitch was given a pair of evil sidekicks, the eerie eels known wittily as Flotsam and Jetsam. Ursula herself, conceived as the latest in a long line of Disney villainesses, owed a good deal of her size, shape, and demeanor to the 400-pound male actor known as Divine who starred as a woman in numerous films (including the original *Hairspray*) by John Waters, a friend of Ashman's from Baltimore. (So tied to Divine is the origin of Ursula that there was a rumor in New York during the casting of the stage *Little Mermaid* that Disney was going to hire a man for the role, which Disney Theatrical's president, Thomas Schumacher, says is not out of the question in the future.)

Clearly the humor was running a bit more sophisticated than the much cozier banter of, say, Thumper and Flower in *Bambi* or Jock and Trusty in *Lady and the Tramp*. The expansion of the Disney humor palette gave adults something to enjoy while the kids in the house were enthralled by the action. Here was Disney with an updated, hipper edge, and audiences clearly responded.

The film won Oscars for its Alan Menken score and for best song ("Under the Sea") for Menken and Ashman. ("Kiss the Girl" was also nominated.) The film reinvigorated Disney animation and resuscitated animation itself as a commercially viable entertainment medium. With *The Little Mermaid*, all the seeds were sown for *Beauty and the Beast*, *Aladdin*, *The Lion King*, and Disney's entire "second classic period," as it is frequently called.

WITHIN A FEW YEARS of the release of *The Little Mermaid*, Disney had entered the Broadway world for real with its 1994 theatrical production of *Beauty and the Beast*, based on the smash-hit 1991 film (*The New York Times* theater critic Frank Rich called that film the best musical of the year). Again the score was written by Alan Menken (three of the songs Menken had written with Howard Ashman for the film had been nominated for Oscars, and "Beauty and the Beast" had won). Sadly, Howard Ashman died of complications related to AIDS in 1991, so the legendary Tim Rice stepped in to write additional lyrics for the expanded Broadway score.

The Lion King followed in 1997, and an original production, *Elton John & Tim Rice's AIDA*, opened in 2000 at The Palace; *Tarzan*, with a score by Phil Collins, made its New York stage debut at the Richard Rodgers Theatre in 2006. As one show followed another, Disney established an entire Broadway division, now called Disney Theatrical Productions, helmed by producer Thomas Schumacher (who had started at Disney in Burbank right around the time the new wave of animated film was beginning).

Among the projects he always had in mind for stage development was *The Little Mermaid*. To him, that film seemed perfect for stage adaptation. "Walt Disney loved music," says Schumacher, "and all of his films rely heavily on their songs and their scores. But *Mermaid* is the first real animated film musical, so the stage version is not just the translation of a film to the stage, it's a translation of a film musical back to the stage."

The highest conceptual hurdle that had to be cleared in remaking *The Little Mermaid* for the stage is that most of the action occurs underwater. Easy in animation. Difficult in a world of three dimensions, real time, and the laws of gravity. And, as Schumacher has always insisted, having a great story is not enough to justify a Disney stage production; there also has to be what he calls "a big idea" about the means of telling that story.

And so Disney Theatrical undertook a search for a powerful theatrical visionary with a big idea for translating *The Little Mermaid* to the stage, with the medium's demands and realities so different from film. The first person Schumacher turned to was British director/choreographer Matthew Bourne, who ascended to international acclaim for his retooling of *Swan Lake* for Sadler's Wells in 1995 (a production in which all the swans were played by men and which has been an international phenomenon).

Bourne went to work on *The Little Mermaid* while Disney continued to pursue other projects for development. At a certain point, however, it became clear that Bourne was headed down a road that was a significant departure from the film, and both Bourne and Disney (in the person of Schumacher) decided the collaboration was not going to work.

"Matthew loved *The Little Mermaid* movie," says Schumacher, "but what he wanted to explore, mostly, was the wondrous tale of Hans Christian Andersen's "Little Mermaid," and that's not what we wanted to do. So rather than either of us trying to persuade the other to change the essential creative direction of the show, we decided to move on to other things." Disney produced *Tarzan* in New York, and Bourne signed on as co-director and co-choreographer of *Mary Poppins*, a joint production of Disney and Cameron Mackintosh, which opened in London in 2004 and New York in 2006.

Schumacher then began talking to the top echelon of Broadway directors, trying to find someone with a staging idea that suited his vision for a theatrical production of *The Little Mermaid*. One of that illustrious group wanted to do the job but told Schumacher that he hadn't seen the original film because he didn't like to watch animation. "Well, you have to watch it about a hundred times before you can go and put it onstage," says the producer. So he passed on the offer and "let it kind of sit there for a year."

OPPOSITE: A studio portrait of actress Sierra Boggess, who originated the role of Ariel in the Broadway *Little Mermaid.*

Schumacher began to despair of finding a director for his show until he had a meeting with Francesca Zambello, a woman who might not have seemed the most likely candidate for the job. An American who grew up in Europe (where she learned French, Italian, German, and Russian), Zambello has earned an international reputation as an opera director capable of combining psychological insight with production innovation. In that male-dominated world, she's worked to much acclaim at the Met, the Bolshoi, the Royal Opera in London, the Paris Opera and in Italy at both La Scala and La Fenice.

She's also directed a substantial number of musicals, from *Showboat* and *Lady in the Dark* in London to *Porgy and Bess* at the Kennedy Center, *Street Scene* in Berlin, and *West Side Story* on a stage floating over an Austrian lake. Recently named a Chevalier des Arts et des Lettres by the French government, she has also received three Olivier Awards and two *Evening Standard* Awards for Best Musical and Best Opera in London.

The producer and director met through opera singer Lauren Flanagan in 1997. Schumacher, who grew up in San Francisco, had returned home to see his old high school friend performing as Yaroslavna in Borodin's *Prince Igor* with the San Francisco Opera. Zambello had directed the production.

"At the dinner after the performance," she remembers, "we were sitting next to each other. We liked each other, and Lauren just said, 'You two will work together.' At that point I was moving more into the music-theater realm for philosophical reasons, because I find a lot of opera too distancing and too elitist and not connected enough to the public of today."

Nothing concrete came of their first meeting, but the paths of the director and producer continued to cross. They spoke of the possibility of her taking on an American production of *The Hunchback of Notre Dame*, which Disney Theatrical had produced in Germany; eventually Schumacher asked Zambello to stage a reading of *Carnival!* (the 1961 film based on the 1953 play *Lili*), which he was considering. Neither production materialized.

Quite separately, Zambello was asked to stage a short Aladdin show for Disneyland, which put her in the orbit of Alan Menken, who had written the music for the Aladdin film. "Then I met Tom again through Alan," Zambello relates, "and Tom just said, 'Why don't we get together and talk about things? I knew that he had been working on *The Little Mermaid* but had not gone forward with it, which I thought was tragic. So I had dinner one night in the summer of 2004. And we had sushi, appropriately enough.

"So I asked him why he had given up on it. Because to me, *The Little Mermaid* is a mythic story," continues Zambello. "It's the story of everyone who has ever wanted to be something they are not, who wanted a life other than the one they are living. Who has never felt out of place in life?

"And he said, 'We haven't found a way to do the water.'"

Now, staging a production "underwater" did not seem all that unsurmountable a problem to Zambello. Certainly such scenic demands are not unknown in the world of opera: every Ring cycle by Wagner has its Rhine Maidens, after all, who are a kind of German, freshwater version of mermaids. "If you come from a world that deals with myth, legend, and lore," Schumacher would later tell the *New Yorker*, "you say, 'Okay, we'll do underwater.'"

"I am a director for whom the story is the most important thing," Zambello says, "so I said, 'I think you just start with the story. The story is so powerful. It's a myth, it's primal, it speaks to everyone, not just to girls but to boys, adults, anyone who has felt themselves ever to be an outsider. And that is part

ABOVE: *Little Mermaid* director Francesca Zambello.
OPPOSITE: Pulitzer Prize–winning playwright Doug Wright, author of the show's book.

of the human psyche—that every one of us is an outsider at some point in our lives, and I said, to me that is the guiding reality of this. And the fact that the story is about this girl is a kind of a jewel. It's a shell, a beautiful metaphor unto itself. So I'd start there rather than worrying about how we were going to swim. Let the jewel-like quality of the world guide us.

"I didn't have an instant solution to the swimming, but I did say that I didn't think it should be highly technical. I said that it should be a musical that uses simple means to convey the underwater world, to engage the audience's fantasy."

"Fundamentally," says Schumacher, "Francesca's big idea was to play the play. And when I said, 'How are you going to make them swim?' she said, 'I'm not. They're going to walk out onstage and tell the story.' And that really was a big idea. I think we had all been working too hard on it to solve it."

The staging solution was not yet fully known, but Schumacher and Zambello were clear on one thing. This production would have no water, no wires, and no flying. The focus would be on the actors telling the story of Ariel, and all the magic of the medium would be brought to bear on telling that story in the most captivating manner possible.

Part of that process would entail reconsidering the book. The stage version of the story would be based on the Hans Christian Andersen original and the Disney film, as written and directed by Ron Clements and John Musker, but it would have entirely new content, as well, some of it to be discovered in the process of making the show. Enter playwright Doug Wright, another unlikely choice for the creative team. Doug Wright received Tony and Drama Desk nominations for his book of the Broadway musical *Grey Gardens*, which gave him considerable credibility in a very specific medium. He won the Tony, the Drama Desk, and a Pulitzer Prize in Drama, to boot, for *I Am My Own Wife* (a nonmusical, fact-based play for one actor who plays some forty roles). Wright also won an Obie for *Quills*, his play about the Marquis de Sade, and wrote the screenplay for the film, which received three Academy Award nominations.

"There were several things I wanted to do with the stage version," Wright summarizes. "One of those was to make it clear that Ariel's longing is not so much for the prince, but for a world in which she feels truly realized on her own terms, and it's important that she voice those aspirations before she even meets a prince. Her ambitions are bigger than any one man." So while both the Andersen original and the Disney film both had statues of handsome young princes, the stage show would not.

Another goal of the stage production was to make Ariel herself as proactive in her story as possible. In the climactic sea battle of the film, Eric sweeps in on his ship and impales Ursula on the prow. In the stage production Ariel becomes the author of her own redemption. She has given up her literal voice for a life with the prince, but finds her real voice—her essence as a living being—through her willingness to reject her personal happiness with Eric to re-establish the rightful order of the sea, with her father as king.

The task of writing new music for the production would go to Alan Menken, who has now won a record-setting eight Oscars for songs composed for Disney animated films. "Well," jokes the *Mermaid* veteran, "I wasn't going to let anyone else do it." To write new lyrics, Menken turned to Glenn Slater, his collaborator on Disney's *Home on the Range*, among other projects. By the time they were done, they had written ten new songs for the show.

In addition to Ariel's new numbers, Prince Eric has two new songs, as does Scuttle and his flock of friends. There are new production numbers, too: a haunting quartet of unmet desire, a slithering duet for Flotsam and Jetsam, and a take-no-prisoners showstopper for Ursula. It's an eclectic score, which is a big part of its fun, adding '60s rock, vaudeville, and '20s Brechtian cabaret to the already diverse mix.

Rehearsals for the Broadway production of *The Little Mermaid* began on May 29, 2007, at the New 42nd Street Studios in the heart of Times Square. The cast had six weeks to learn the basics of the show before it would move to Denver for an out-of-town, pre-Broadway run.

ARIEL'S
part two
CIRCLE

ARIEL

I wanna be where the people are . . .

AT THE CENTER OF OUR STORY, of course, is Ariel, the little mermaid of the title and one of the most beloved characters in the Disney canon. An adolescent creature of the sea, she comes from an indefinite storybook past ("Once upon a time"), but she's also recognizable as a teenager from the present day, and she has an enormous following of youngsters who find their dreams and fantasies are much more to their liking than their day-to-day reality. And many a young woman these days has been named Ariel after her.

Like every good daughter, Ariel loves her father, King Triton, and her six sisters, but—unlike any of the other denizens of the deep—she is obsessed with life above the water. She is also dangerously attracted, her father believes, to "human stuff," which she collects after shipwrecks and stashes in her secret grotto.

Although she doesn't know why, Ariel feels different from everyone around her and completely misunderstood. She feels that the merpeople are trying to force her to be someone she is not. With her good friend, Flounder, she spends her spare time exploring shipwrecks and visiting the surface of the ocean to get a glimpse of passing boats—and the humans who sail on them—taking much of her (mis)information from a somewhat confused seagull named Scuttle.

Ariel is attractive, charming, resourceful, courageous, affectionate, and loyal. She's also headstrong, rash, impatient, petulant, and defiant. In other words, she is young. Like many human teens, she is anxious for the freedom that comes with adulthood—and finding true love—even though she understands freedom, adulthood, and love only imperfectly.

The Broadway Ariel was created by a young actress by the name of Sierra Boggess, who herself has been a lifelong fan of *The Little Mermaid*, which she first saw as a very young girl. What does she like about Ariel? "Her spirit, her positive nature, her yearning, her passion—all these fantastic things—that she goes after what she wants, because where she is in life isn't enough for her. And that's how she feels: she has to be human, she has to have legs, and she will arrive one day. It isn't a question of if, it's when, and that's so cool."

The Little Mermaid is the story of Ariel's transformation from childhood to adulthood, from an individual who puts her own happiness first to one who thinks first of duty. Like many a royal character before her, she comes to see beyond her own needs to those of her kingdom and its subjects, including her family. At the beginning of the story she is King Triton's daughter; at the end, after the trials and tribulations of her great adventure on land, she becomes fully herself, both a princess and a strong young woman of enormous potential in her own right. And if that's not enough, she's even managed to find her heart's true love.

OPPOSITE: Ariel (Sierra Boggess) enjoys a bath in Prince Eric's palace. ABOVE: A costume sketch for the legged Ariel.

KING TRITON

I can govern a kingdom,
but I can't control my own daughter.

ARIEL'S FATHER IS THE KING of the sea. The widowed monarch loves all his daughters, but there's a special place in his heart for his youngest. Triton, a figure out of classic mythology, is a benevolent if forceful king who rules his domain with kindness and understanding when possible, with an iron will when necessary. If only he could understand his daughter! A talented singer, like her sisters, Ariel's voice most resembles that of the late queen, whom Triton misses deeply, but his youngest just won't keep her mind on her music lessons. She is obsessed with humans and spends all her time at the surface, defying her father's own orders.

Triton wants Ariel to be happy. He is, however, as protective as any good father and wants to keep his daughter out of harm's way. He is adamant that he will not lose her the same way he lost his queen—by human hands. Triton is torn between his key social role as ruler and his personal life as a doting father. He finds himself frustrated, wishing his daughter to love him more than fear him. He knows she must someday go her own way in the world, but he fears that she is not yet ready.

"I think that in the show, Triton and Ariel have a closer father-daughter relationship than in the movie, or in the Hans Christian Andersen story," says Norm Lewis, who first essayed the Broadway role of Triton. "There's a closer connection. And he's purposefully less kingly. In the film Triton always wears his crown. For the stage version he only wears it for public functions, not when he's alone with Ariel. He's much less a Greek or Roman god and much more a father. And the hard thing was maintaining that balance between leadership and tenderness." So the quartet, "If Only" is quite poignant for Triton. He is willing to give up his life for his daughter, but it's deeply emotional for him—as it is to fathers in the audience—to let her go and marry Prince Eric.

ABOVE: A concept sketch for King Triton.
OPPOSITE: Triton in the final version of his costume.

Norm Lewis, as King Triton, and Bret Shuford

URSULA

Don't be shy, Ariel, darling. It's me — your Auntie Ursula!

WALT DISNEY INTRODUCED HIS FIRST no-holds-barred villain in his first animated feature, *Snow White and the Seven Dwarfs*, in 1937. Over the years, the Evil Queen has been joined by Maleficent, Cruella De Vil, and others, from Captain Hook and Jafar to Hades and Simba's craven Uncle Scar. Yet none, perhaps, is as malignant as Ursula, the shape-shifting sea demon in *The Little Mermaid*. This is one very unpleasant cephalopod. Her cyanide-blue skin alone should say "keep away" to any curious denizens of the deep.

In the stage show, Ursula is portrayed as King Triton's sister, banished by Triton for using her powers for evil instead of good. She resents Triton for having inherited the larger share of the ocean realm from their father, Poseidon, and she wants it all for herself. In her new song, "I Want the Good Times Back," a paean to greed, Ursula struts her comic-villain stuff, belting out her ruthless envy like a crazed cabaret singer who may just have had too much fermented seaweed at happy hour.

For Sheri Rene Scott, who created the role for the Broadway version of *The Little Mermaid*, Ursula is a juggling act. For one thing, there is her enormous costume with its flowing tentacles. And just how satanic can this character be? She's evil, sure, but the character shouldn't frighten the children in the audience so much that they can't enjoy the show. Scott settled for an image of Ursula that owes something significant to Norma Desmond as played by Gloria Swanson in *Sunset Boulevard*. She's a sharp cockle, too, able to wrap her traplike mind around schemes to satisfy her enormous appetitive entitlement.

The brother-sister, aunt-niece relationship is new, but it had been included in the film, in a lyric for "Fathoms Below" that was cut to trim some minutes off the film. It had been the only reference to the family relationship in the film. Like Greek myths, where unsuspecting mortals sometimes become enmeshed in the jealousies of the gods, family relationships tend to heighten the stakes. When it's all in the family, everything is personal.

According to Scott, Ursula feels "very, very wronged, but she's incredibly self-righteous. And we've seen in real life just how deadly that combination can be."

When Ursula tells Ariel that they are much alike, she is not mistaken: they are both strong women. But Ursula has allowed herself to be twisted into becoming cruel and evil; Ariel does not want to lose her decency and kindness in order to be strong.

OPPOSITE: Ursula (Sherie Rene Scott), Ariel's villainous aunt, with her magic shell. ABOVE: A development sketch for Ursula's costume.

PRINCE ERIC

Follow that voice — to the ends of the earth if we have to.

EVERY FAIRY-TALE PRINCESS MUST FIND her heart's desire, and Ariel's charmer is Prince Eric. Eric has lost both his parents and is coming of age under the guidance of a majordomo named Grimsby, who is determined that Prince Eric will marry by the time of his next birthday and assume the throne of his kingdom, as his father wished.

But Eric has other ideas. Just as Ariel is drawn to land, Eric thrives on the sea. He has no interest in being tied to a kingdom on the shore. He just wants to sail out on the ocean, which is where he feels most alive.

Of all the changes made between the film and stage versions, perhaps Eric was changed the most, and those changes were triggered by the notion that Ariel should be the architect of her own fate and her own rescue. While Eric was perfectly likable in the film, the two young people fall in love on first sight not because of anything either has done to impress the other with their characters.

The Broadway *Little Mermaid*, with its more self-determining Ariel, needed an Eric who deserves her more. Anyone Ariel falls in love with has to be more than a pretty face with a castle. Now, however, Eric falls in love with something he sees in Ariel, not just her voice. Eric has become far more perceptive. He loves Ariel even when she can't speak, and he realizes it.

Prince Eric has two big new numbers for the stage production. The first, in act one, is called "Her Voice," a rapturous hymn to Ariel and Eric's first wild wave of love.

"A lot of Eric's process happens offstage," says Sean Palmer, who originated the Broadway role. "You have to assume he's been going through some kind of turmoil. He's been staring at the sea for weeks and driving himself crazy looking for Ariel. And then he comes in and pours it all out in 'Her Voice.'"

In the second-act song, "One Step Closer," in which Eric teaches Ariel to dance, he begins to really understand the depth of his feelings for her as he teaches, and he learns that there are ways of communicating that don't involve speaking.

"Eric has a much larger heart in the stage version," says Palmer. "I don't think you get that in the film as much. You get his desire, but you don't get his heart. I mean, he's warm and charming, but with the show we really follow the two of them as they're coming to terms with love and growing up and asserting themselves away from their families."

And so when Ariel and Eric marry at the end of the show, the audience feels a great sense of satisfaction, both in the romantic sense (of the traditional fairy tale) and the somewhat more modern notion that the two of them are a perfect fit.

ABOVE: Prince Eric's wedding-costume sketch. OPPOSITE: The prince (Sean Palmer) in less formal fairy-tale attire.

SEBASTIAN

Life under the sea is better than anything they got up there!

IF ANY CARTOON CHARACTER can be said to achieve fame, the claim can certainly be made by the cantankerous Sebastian, who is not just red-faced with frustration as Ariel's music teacher and guardian, but red from the tip of his antennae to the nippers on his numerous claws. Like a true crab, this musical member of the exoskeletal clan is crusty on the outside but soft and sweet inside, especially where Ariel is concerned. He tries to be strict, for her own good, but his heart melts like drawn butter when he realizes how unhappy she is. Escaping from a mad seafood-obsessed Chef Louis on land, Sebastian becomes an advocate of Ariel's liaison with Price Eric, because, like a good parent, he wants for her what will make her happy.

Like the film Sebastian (which was voiced by Samuel E. Wright, who later debuted as Mufasa in Disney's stage version of *The Lion King*), the stage Sebastian speaks with a pronounced Jamaican accent that suits the calypso beat of "Under the Sea," possibly the audience's favorite song from the film. As in the film, the stage Sebastian sings "Under the Sea" and "Kiss the Girl." He is also part of the new act two quartet, "If Only," sung by Ariel, Eric, King Triton, and himself.

In the film, Sebastian is a tiny little crab, able to sit on a mermaid's shoulder. On stage, Sebastian is played by an adult male (Tituss Burgess originating the role), which means he is a much larger physical presence. Like King Triton, he is sure he knows that what she wants for herself is not good for her, but when he sees her with the prince, he mellows, and comes to understand that his job is to help her attain happiness on her own terms.

In the animated *Little Mermaid*, Sebastian skittles around on the ends of his pincers a lot. In real life, moving like a crab for two hours is a lot more difficult, even if the movement is only meant to be suggestive rather than literal. Tituss Burgess admits he is not really a dancer and gives a lot of the credit for his portrayal of Sebastian to choreographer Stephen Mear, who helped him work out the movement style.

Another daunting task? Stepping into Samuel Wright's role. "Well there's no re-creating that!" says Burgess," so I didn't try. For one thing my voice is much higher. I didn't even try to copy Sam Wright's accent. I just worked with a dialect coach until it was right for me."

OPPOSITE: Sebastian (Tituss Burgess) wears a bigger hat than depicted in the sketch (above); his vest is now red, the legs simplified.

SCUTTLE

With proper dinglehopper groomin',
rest assured — you'll look real human.

SCUTTLE IS ARIEL'S BEST above-water friend and her chief source of information about humans. Through Scuttle, Ariel learns all about the artifacts she collects and hides in her secret grotto—not knowing, of course, that the somewhat birdbrained Scuttle's got it all wrong. Scuttle tells Ariel that a serving fork is a dinglehopper, just right for dressing her hair, and that tobacco pipes are musical instruments called snarf-blatts. In the movie, Scuttle (voiced by comedian Buddy Hackett) only gets to speak his lines; for the show, he has two new songs. The first, backed up by a trio of fellow gulls, is "Human Stuff."

Scuttle speaks in a highfalutin' manner that he only half understands (he, too, would like to be something he isn't). With his roots in Roman comic drama—the source of Western comedic tradition—he's a familiar character from the works of Shakespeare to the early days of film to today's sitcoms. Like Mrs. Malaprop in Sheridan's *The Rivals* (1775), Scuttle murders the language, and like Leo Gorcey in the old black-and-white Bowery Boys movies, he does it in a woikin' class New Yawk accent.

Broadway veteran Eddie Korbich, who likens Scuttle to Ariel's "goofy uncle," studied the movements of real seagulls before setting his role as Scuttle and considers his performance a tribute to Brooklyn-born Buddy Hackett. The actor also put his own stamp on the finished *Little Mermaid*. "Positoovity" was not originally conceived as such an elaborate tap number, but Korbich can tap up a storm, so choreographer Stephen Mear, who helped create "Step in Time," the stunning tap number in *Mary Poppins*, made use of that talent.

Streetwise Scuttle may not be the swiftest seagull in the flock, but he's loyal and loving and would do anything for Ariel, including teaching her to walk and bucking up her confidence with his new second-act number "Positoovity," during which he and his feathered flock kick up their heels in one the show's crowd-pleasing numbers. A stock character from the world of vaudeville, Scuttle helps keep the humor of the show percolating.

ABOVE AND OPPOSITE: The costume for Scuttle (Eddie Korbich) changed the most between the Denver tryout and the Broadway premiere.

FLOUNDER

It's true. I'm a guppy — a total guppy.

IF SCUTTLE IS ARIEL'S goofy uncle, then her little friend Flounder is like a favorite kid brother who tags along behind her, which is okay with Ariel. Flounder, who's pretty much afraid of his own shadow, is at his bravest when he's with Ariel, and for her he is capable of great valor. The trouble is he is so honest that he keeps giving away their secret excursions to the surface without even meaning to, continually getting Ariel in trouble. He finds himself torn between his love for Ariel and his duty to see that she is safe and protected.

Despite his name, Flounder is portrayed as a playful yellow-and-blue reef fish (a real flounder is a gray fish with both of its eyes on the same side of its flat body). Unlike in the film, the stage Flounder sings, along with Ariel's sisters, a new '60s pop song, "She's in Love," in which he realizes that Ariel is in love with the prince.

As fate would have it, the two young actors who rotated in the role of Flounder all through the rehearsal process and the Denver tryout—Cody Hanford and J.J. Singleton—were too old for the role by the time the show opened. They were not only getting taller, but their voices were changing, so they could no longer sing the score in the right key. They were replaced by a new pair of young actors (Trevor Braun and Brian D'Addario) and attended opening night as members of the audience (both had already been cast in new shows). At the first listening party for the cast album of the show, Flounder's "She's in Love" was played four times—each time with a different boy's voice—and each boy received a CD containing their own version of the song.

OPPOSITE: J.J. Singleton as Flounder in the pre-Broadway run of *The Little Mermaid*. ABOVE: Two sketches for Flounder's costume.

FLOTSAM & JETSAM

DISNEY'S HEROES AND HEROINES always have their sidekicks. Ariel has Scuttle, Flounder, and Sebastian. Sometimes the villains have them, too, only they are usually referred to as minions. Ursula has a pair of electric eels named Flotsam and Jetsam whom she adores and tortures in equal measure. They are not actually related to Ariel, but as Aunt Ursula's creatures, they play something of the role of evil cousins. In the film, both characters were voiced by the actress Paddi Edwards; onstage Flotsam and Jetsam are played by men (Tyler Maynard and Derrick Baskin in the original cast) with an almost supernatural attachment and a single purpose: to do Ursula's bidding.

Expanded for the show, the characters of Flotsam and Jetsam developed in Doug Wright's book into a supersmooth saltwater version of Si and Am in *Lady and the Tramp*. They are evil, to be sure, but there's a mischievousness about them that makes us watch them with a certain glee (maybe because they are able to do the kinds of things the rest of us only wish we could in our worst moments). They manage to be entirely seductive, especially in their deadly duet, "Sweet Child," a hypnotic anthem of disingenuousness that fools the guileless Ariel totally.

OPPOSITE: Flotsam (Tyler Maynard) and Jetsam (Derrick Baskin) cook up a stew of trouble.
ABOVE: The evil eels were first sketched as gangsters, complete with fedoras.

GRIMSBY

LIKE SEBASTIAN, Grimsby is a bit crusty on the outside but warm and toasty inside. He's the only father figure Prince Eric has and, like Triton, he's trying to get the youngster in his care to do what is right while loving the lad like his own son. It's Grimsby's task to get Eric married by his impending birthday. Grimsby, who accompanies Eric on his frequent sails upon the briny (despite his own tendency to be seasick), comes up with the idea of a singing contest when Eric says he's fallen in love with a voice. To create the expanded role on Broadway, Disney turned to an old friend, Jonathan Freeman, who has a pretty famous voice of his own: he played the sonorous villain Jafar in *Aladdin* and its sequels and also did a turn as Cogsworth, the clock, in *Beauty and the Beast* onstage.

CARLOTTA

EVERY CASTLE NEEDS a good-hearted head housekeeper, and Eric's chateau has Carlotta, who instantly takes charge of Ariel and provides her with all the things she thinks a young girl needs. She is motherly toward Ariel and treats her with great affection but does not see her as a realistic choice as a wife for Prince Eric. Carlotta was originated on Broadway by actress Heidi Blickenstaff (who also served as an understudy to Ursula).

CHEF LOUIS

PART OF THE SUCCESS of *The Little Mermaid* film was its cast of eccentric secondary characters, among them seafood chef Louis, who never met a bouillabaisse he didn't love. Another stock comic character, Louis is so memorable from his big "Les Poissons" number in the film, it would have been a crime against audience expectations to leave him out of the show. And since we're having Louis, we might as well have a gigantic production number, too, with Sebastian running around and hiding from a singing and dancing chorus of sous chefs carrying fish-laden salvers to the dinner table. The first Chef Louis on Broadway was John Treacy Egan, who came to *The Little Mermaid* from *The Producers*, where he had not only starred as Max Bialystock, but had also played two other major roles, Roger DeBris and Franz Liebkind!

THIS PAGE: Costume sketches for the members of Prince Eric's "family."
OPPOSITE, CLOCKWISE FROM TOP LEFT: Jonathan Freeman, Heidi Blickenstaff, and John Treacy Egan.

MERSISTERS

IN HANS CHRISTIAN ANDERSEN'S story, the little mermaid is the youngest of six sisters. Disney's film made her the youngest of seven (one mermaid for each of the seven seas, perhaps). Ariel's six older sisters—Aquata, Andrina, Arista, Atina, Adella, and Alana—are as alike as they are different. Each has her own personality (and her own special mode of singing); together they represent the norm that Ariel feels estranged from.

Her sisters fulfill their roles as princesses without challenging the status quo. They do what is expected of them and, as far as Ariel can tell, they make her father happy. She is the odd mermaid out, even though it's clear that she loves her sisters and that they love her. They just don't understand Ariel, and because she's the youngest in the family, they tend to baby her. And besides, raising Ariel is not their job.

Alan Menken and Glenn Slater wrote the sisters a new song for the stage version, which gave the score another musical layer. What could be more natural than six sassy sisters performing as a group of Sixties-style singers? Ariel's sextet of siblings brings perfect period sound to "She's in Love." To portray the sisters, Disney chose Cathryn Basile (Arista), Cicily Daniels (Allana), Michelle Lookadoo (Adella), Zakiya Young Mizen (Atina), Chelsea Morgan Stock (Andrina), and Kay Trinidad (Aquata). These young women play many roles in the course of a single performance.

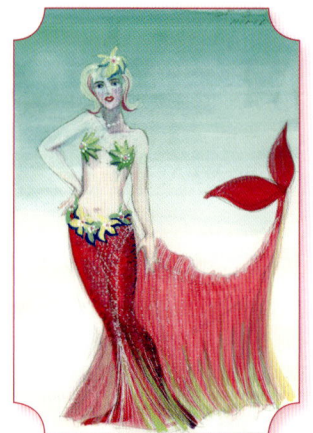

THIS PAGE: Costume sketches for Ariel's six singing sisters. OPPOSITE: The six princesses with their father, King Triton.

Tails of the Sea

NOT ALL MERMAID TAILS are created equal. There are three different tail sizes in *The Little Mermaid*. Ariel, as leading lady, has the biggest fins; her six sisters have two smaller versions (based on the height of the actress). All of them were built by Michael Curry, who also produced masks and puppets for *The Lion King*, on a sprung-steel rod that snaps into what the costume team calls an "industrial panty." The tails are given tension as well as mobility by a kind of bungee cord; these must occasionally be tightened and replaced so the tails don't become too flaccid. The "cage" of the tail is then partly covered in a light organza fabric, which is painted and beaded and trimmed with ribbon. (Rehearsal tails were made of the kind of foam used in air-conditioning systems.)

Ariel's tail was originally built with a motor in it that allowed her fluke to flutter independently of the rest of the piece (which required a technician to cue the movements). Unfortunately, the mechanics made the tail both heavy and loud, neither of which was helpful to a mermaid who sings and dances on wheels. So the idea was abandoned in favor of old-fashioned physical movements that are controlled by the actresses wearing them. Choreographers, however, take note: an actress in a tail has a wide turning radius; plan pirouettes with caution!

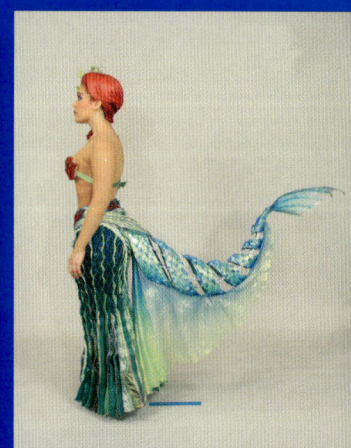

TOP: The creative staff takes a close look at Ariel's tail in Denver.
RIGHT AND OPPOSITE: Costume "bible" portraits of the seven daughters (Michelle Lookadoo, Cathryn Basile, Sierra Boggess, Zakiya Young Mizen, Kay Trinidad, Chelsea Morgan Stock, Cicily Daniels).

ABOVE: For rehearsals, the mersisters wore temporary tails made of structured air-conditioning foam.
BELOW: An early version of Ariel's tail.

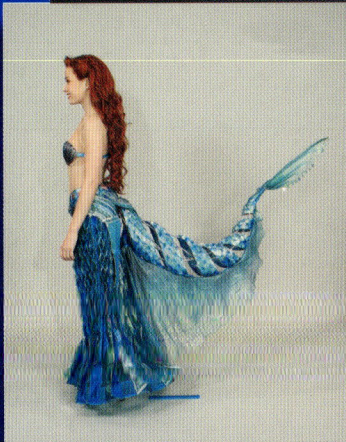

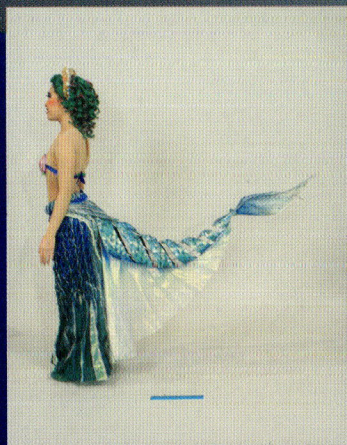

ARIEL'S
part three
VOICE

OPPOSITE: Sierra Boggess rehearses "Part of Your World."

HOWEVER DIFFERENT THE versions of Andersen's "Little Mermaid" may be—and however different all the various mermaid stories are from cultures all over the world—one thing is consistent: central to the story is the mermaid's voice. And true to this fundamental component of the story, what we hear first about Ariel is how magnificent her voice is.

Certainly, it's Ariel's voice that first captures Prince Eric's imagination. "Follow that voice," he orders his crew, "to the ends of the earth if we have to." Next comes Sebastian, her music tutor, who exclaims to Ariel's father, King Triton: "Such a voice, that child!" Her sisters, too, are impressed, singing:

> And then there is the youngest
> In her musical debut:
> Our seventh little sister—
> We're presenting her to you
> To sing a song Sebastian wrote.
> Her voice is like a bell.
> It's our sister, Ariel. . . .

Even Flotsam and Jetsam have heard about Ariel's famous talent, so when Ursula tells them she wants Triton's youngest daughter, Flotsam asks, "The one with the beautiful voice?" King Triton, too, addresses his daughter's vocal abilities: "You've been given a gift," he reminds her, "your mother's voice. It's a wondrous talent, one that demands stewardship and care."

Naturally, it is just this perfect, character-defining voice that Ursula demands from Ariel as the price for her legs and a chance to marry Prince Eric. But Ariel's voice is both a fact—she sings beautifully—and a metaphor: her voice is who she is, or is it?

Everyone is so concerned with Ariel's voice that they may be missing who she really is, which is far more varied, complete, and complex than her voice alone. Clearly, her voice is not so precious to Ariel. she's willing to sacrifice it in order to live on land and win her prince.

OPPOSITE: Sierra Boggess performs "Part of Your World."

But the concept of Ariel's voice is even bigger than who she is (as we see in her relationship with Ursula): it is the notion of each individual—and each woman in particular—having a say in her own destiny, of being self-determined rather than determined by others. Little Ariel wants to decide what her life will be like for herself, not to stand obediently by and let others decide for her. She really is like Ursula in one way: they are both "gals with ambition."

There is yet another layer in which we speak of Ariel's voice, and that is the notion that the story itself is Ariel's voice, because it tells her tale. It is the means by which her story is expressed to the world. And in the theater, every aspect of the production is brought to bear on the telling of her story. Most specifically, of course, in the case of *The Little Mermaid*, are the words of the text and songs, and the music itself. These are the means that Ariel has of voicing her own personality and that the production has of presenting her journey.

As for the words of the story, that task would fall largely to Pulitzer Prize–winning author Doug Wright. To him would fall the responsibility of the book. Now, the book of a Broadway show is a complex, collaborative, evolving, and fluid thing. The playwright works with the director, the composer and lyricist, the choreographer, and others on creating the structure of the show itself as well as many of the additional details of storytelling.

In working out the structure, the writer and his colleagues decide how the story will be told and how each beat of the story will be realized: Dialogue? Song? Dance? Or some combination of these things? And then, of course, the writer must provide the words themselves. Sometimes the book writer even writes the song lyrics, but in this case, Wright's singular, enormous contribution was the script itself.

Prince Eric (Sean Palmer) longs for a life at sea and is mesmerized by the sound of Ariel's voice.

propel Ariel as the real protagonist, that the action was happening to her rather than being instigated by her. I felt that, like most protagonists, she had to be empowered. I think that's a big message in the piece—that she creates her own dilemma and resolves it. The way she saves her father and gets the guy herself is a message that I wanted to convey to young women.

"Tom [Schumacher] and I talked about a number of different writers," says Zambello. "I respected Doug Wright's work, but he's not the first person you'd pick up on your radar in thinking of a writer for *The Little Mermaid*. Then I met him and saw his kind of Southern gentility, his love for fable, and his central notion as a writer, that everything is character-driven, and I understood why he should write this show."

Happily, Wright understood Zambello's reservations from the beginning. In fact, he actively pursued getting the assignment. "Tom had seen my work," says Wright, "and invited me in for a general meeting, just to talk about potential projects we might do together. And I guess I was in an especially brash mood that morning, because I brought up *The Little Mermaid*. I said, 'with the amazing success you've had with *The Lion King* and *Beauty and the Beast*, it's curious to me that we haven't seen *The Little Mermaid*, because, truthfully, it's my favorite.'

"And he said, 'Well it's interesting that you should bring that up, because we just started work with a very exciting director, Francesca Zambello, and the project is gaining some momentum here, and we happen to be in need of a book writer.' And so my heart soared, and I said, 'As atypical as it may sound, compared to the rest of my work, it's something I'd deeply love to try. And Tom was brave enough to give me the opportunity."

Now, the Opening Night script, as the final version is called, differs radically from what is known as the First Rehearsal script, which, as the name explains, is the script that is handed out to the cast and crew at the first rehearsal. This version of the script is more like a blueprint than a completed piece of literary architecture, but it is far from a first draft. In the case of *The Little Mermaid*, the producer, director, playwright, composer, and lyricist (among others) had been working for as long as five years before the first rehearsal in May 2007.

In fact, when director Francesca Zambello started working on *The Little Mermaid* in 2004, the state of the script as developed to that point by the earlier creative team was one of her major apprehensions. "I was very concerned about the state of the script," she remembers, "that the story did not

To fashion a script, Wright ignored the draft from the first development period and went back to the Hans Christian Andersen story and the animated Disney film. "I felt it was important to start fresh," he says, "to really look at Andersen and really look at the film as my starting points. So, the only prior material I read was the original story and the screenplay by Ron Clements and John Musker for the Disney version. Those were my starting points.

"One of the first things I had to do was to place Andersen's story in the context of its time and compare that to our own times. Obviously, the original story was written for a different age. Andersen grew up in a very repressive and homogeneous environment, and he felt himself as something of an outsider within it. And his "Little Mermaid" expresses some of those same ambitions to grow beyond a world that she as the character and he as the author feel to be mired in conformity.

> **"I felt that, like most protagonists, [Ariel] had to be empowered. I think that's a big message in the piece—that she creates her own dilemma and resolves it."**
> —FRANCESCA ZAMBELLO

"I think it's clear that anyone who had those impulses or feelings in those days was often severely punished for them. Certainly, women in that era were expected to subjugate themselves to men, and that's what Andersen's little mermaid does: she gives herself up for the love of the prince. When you approach the material in the twenty-first century, you have to speak to an entirely different culture.

"In our times, we like to hope that young women with ambition are rewarded for it, not punished, that they can have their own dreams and autonomy independent of the men who may fulfill their romantic lives. So telling the story in this day and age, we want to reward Ariel for the very appetites that bring her so much grief in the original tale.

"Now, I'm an enormous fan of the film, and I think it handles Ariel's journey quite artfully, but there were a few things I wanted to ensure that we did in the stage version. One of those was to make clear that first and foremost Ariel's essential longing isn't for the prince per se. Ariel's longing is for a world where she feels complete and feels at home and feels truly realized on her own terms. And so it's very important to us that she voice those aspirations before she ever even meets a prince.

"And then, along the way, as she embarks on her quest, she meets the prince, and he comes to represent the things she holds closest to her heart. All of us felt it was very important that her ambitions be larger than any one man, than snagging a boyfriend. We wanted to make sure that the goal of her journey was becoming herself. That was critical to me.

"Another was that, when she did meet the prince, he be truly worthy of her. The film is much shorter than our show, and so we had a thrilling opportunity to expand on certain motifs that were in the movie. I wanted to create an Eric who is truly worth Ariel's affection. He's not simply the beautiful face or the handsome statue that we meet in the movie.

Director Francesca Zambello in rehearsal in New York prior to the Denver tryout.

"So we created a prince who has his own issues about growing up and finding his place in the world. He has the incredible pressure of ascending to the throne, when his heart belongs out on the open sea, sailing in his beloved ship. By meeting Ariel, and falling in love not just with her singing voice but with her essential being, he, too, is able to grow into himself, and finally, by the end of the piece, to accept adult responsibility.

"We wanted to be faithful to the film in spirit, but sometimes the best way to serve a movie in adapting it for the stage is to actually change it to serve what works well on the stage. And that's one kind of homage." —DOUG WRIGHT

"The third goal in making Ariel as rich as possible was to ensure that she conquer Ursula herself. We felt that the dramatic antagonists were Ariel and Ursula, so that the final showdown had to be between them, and that Ariel should rescue herself. And that was something that we worked very hard to achieve."

ABOVE: Book writer Doug Wright. To retell the love story, Wright chose to create a more complex, more worthy Eric.

So when Ursula says that she and Ariel are a lot alike—a line that gets an audience laugh at every performance for its absurdity—she's not completely wrong, at least in one sense. "Ursula's tragic flaw isn't her ambition or her desire to succeed," says Wright, "It's the means she employs to achieve her ambitions that are diabolical. Ariel has all the same desires. Yet she's able to leave joy in her wake instead of heartbreak and trauma. The two women are truly linked; it's their methods that render them so different."

And so it seems natural that the two should be related. Wright also recalls that in his earliest drafts he invoked the great jealousies of the gods of Greek mythology in casting Ursula as the sister of Triton. He then discovered that Clements and Muster had made the same emendation to the Andersen story in their prep work for the film. "That convinced me we were on the right track," he says. "It felt like a really juicy element," he continues, "because suddenly, a story of disparate people becomes a story of family dynamics. In a family situation, nothing is abstract, everything is personal."

What Wright found in his theatrical family—Schumacher, Zambello, Menken, et al—was a shared love of the original material. "We wanted to be faithful to the film in spirit, but sometimes the best way to serve a movie in adapting it for the stage is to actually change it to serve what works well on the stage. And that's one kind of homage. There were certain things that we had to change. I mean, we had the opportunity to expand plot lines and beef up the character complexity because we had more stage time, but there were some things that the film does that we simply could not achieve onstage, and so we tried to come up with correlatives."

So there is no sheepdog and no statue of the prince, no Vanessa (the seductive, beautiful form of the protean Ursula), no final chase at sea, and Ursula does not grow to enormous proportions to engulf the ship. But the audience's memories of an original Disney film are vivid, and trying to accommodate their recollections and to balance them against the right of any audience to be surprised by something new is part of the script-development process.

Sierra Boggess and Sean Palmer

THIS PAGE: While many scenes and their characters appeared in the show just as they had in the film, others were cut entirely.

Sierra Boggess and Eddie Korbich

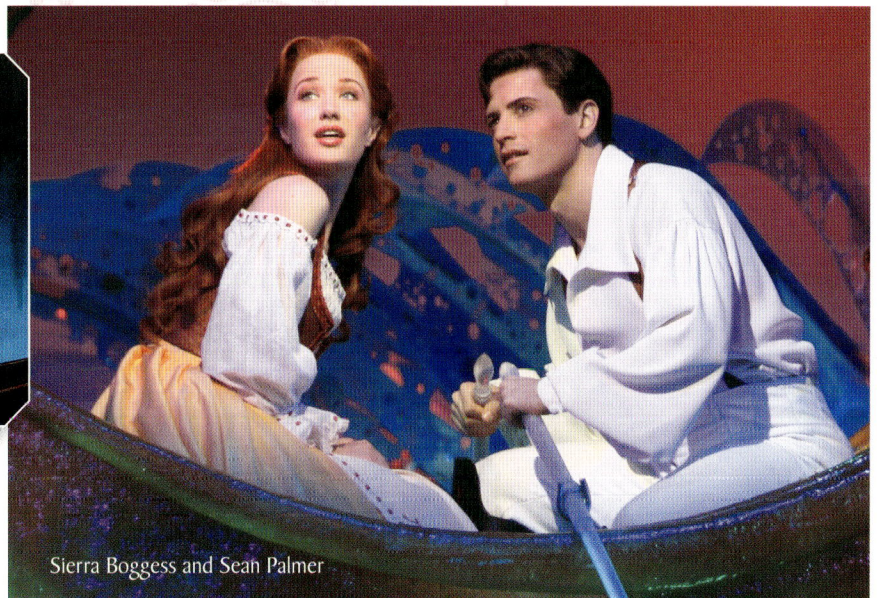

Sierra Boggess and Sean Palmer

One of the most obvious differences between *The Little Mermaid* film and its Broadway cousin is in the number of songs in the score: the show has ten more songs than the film.

"When I joined the project," says Doug Wright, "because it had been in development previously, there were already a number of new songs that had been written. I think 'She's in Love,' had been written, possibly 'Her Voice,' but there were other songs that either didn't exist or could have been better. And as I introduced a new structure into the proceedings, Alan [Menken] and Glenn [Slater] were very cooperative moving songs and trying out altogether new songs. I think 'One Step Closer' was a result of our work together. And I believe that 'I Want the Good Times Back' was something we all arrived at collectively. So, I inherited a number of songs and then we forged a few together as well.

"One thing I felt was that it was almost like my role to be a kind of jeweler. I had all these gorgeous, precious gems—which are songs—and I had to create a setting for them. And as a book writer, you want that setting to be persuasive and extremely economical. I mean, if at the end of the day, fifteen percent of the show is book, and eighty-five percent of it is music, and you can follow every major plot point, then I've done my job."

Balancing the book and the music is ultimately the responsibility of the director, and in this case, she had her eye tightly focused on the process, but she also had a lot of faith in her collaborators. "In any musical," she says, "you have to have the structure in place, which is the book. You have to have the spine; you have to have the skeleton. If you don't have that right, a musical will fail. A lot of musicals have had amazing music, but if the trunk is wrong, the branches don't hang right on the tree. And we worked on making the story that strong spine, so the music shifted around a lot. But Alan was very flexible, and he and Glenn are able to turn things around extremely quickly."

DISNEY'S *THE LITTLE MERMAID* was the first film that composer Alan Menken worked on, and it was a stunning success. The score won an Oscar and so did "Under the Sea." Over the next score of years, Menken would become one of the best-known songwriters in the country—as evidenced by his countless industry awards, including eight Academy Awards and numerous Golden Globes and Grammys, and his recent induction into the Songwriters Hall of Fame. Much of his popularity and renown is related to his work on Disney films.

Menken's music has graced such animated classics as *Beauty and the Beast, Aladdin, Pocahontas, The Hunchback of Notre Dame*, and *Hercules*—for which films he's won eight Academy Awards out of eighteen nominations. Disney opened its renovated New Amsterdam Theater in New York with his *King David* oratorio; his previous Disney collaboration with Glenn Slater, *Home on the Range*, featured vocals by k.d. lang, Bonnie Raitt, and Tim McGraw; three of the songs he wrote with frequent collaborator Stephen Schwartz for the 2007 Disney animated/live-action film *Enchanted* were nominated for an Academy Award in a single year. He's written other Broadway shows, too, including the perennial *A Christmas Carol* and the forthcoming *Sister Act*, among many other projects.

Alan Menken in 1989 and now, having won eight Oscars for the music he's written for Disney films.

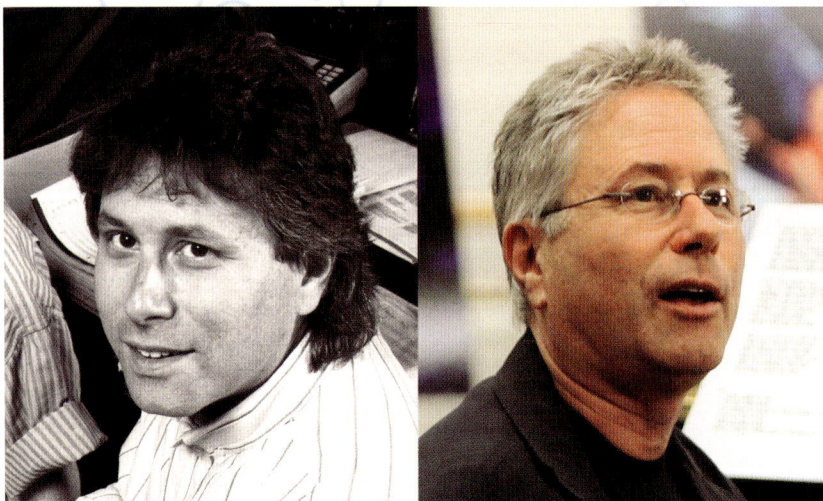

In Denver, director Francesca Zambello explains
her thinking to (from left) lyricist Glenn Slater,
book writer Doug Wright, composer Alan Menken,
and producer Thomas Schumacher.

So there wasn't any question that *The Little Mermaid* musical would call on his talents once again. And he's been in on the project from the beginning, nearly ten years. One of the first decisions was to include all the songs from the film and not to change them significantly. "Well," says Menken, "*The Little Mermaid* film is structured very close to a traditional musical comedy, meaning it's very economical, very tight, and the songs are specific to the story points." Besides, the songs are good, and everyone knows them.

"Howard Ashman's not here to defend his work," says Menken of his former colleague and collaborator, "but he would have been the first one to say we had to adapt it. Still, there were very few cases where I considered it justified to make changes. We changed a pronoun here and there for the sake of the choreography. We had to open up a musical phrase in 'Under the Sea.' Little things. The numbers we broke into with dialogue were mainly the comedy songs, the vaudeville kind of numbers."

"'Fathoms Below' opened up quite a bit. The first part is a section of what Howard and I wrote for the movie, and the second part is what Glenn and I wrote for the show. There was a small structural change to 'Poor Unfortunate Souls,' which now has a kind of faux button for Ursula, and we resurrected a second verse of 'Daughters of Triton' that had been cut from the movie due to time."

Menken and Slater wrote much of the new material for the stage version before Francesca Zambello and Doug Wright came on board the project in 2004. "'The World Above' was written when we were working with Matthew Bourne," Menken recalls, "and we had written a song for Ursula called 'Wasting Away,' which we eventually decided to drop. 'Her Voice' was there; 'She's in Love' was there. At least half the new material."

Howard Ashman in 1989

"He was probably the best talent of our generation, and he didn't wear it on his sleeve. He was a temperamental, wiry, pushy, adorably wonderful, smart, loving person. And he just loved musical theater.

—ALAN MENKEN ON HOWARD ASHMAN

In the course of the musical development, the collaboration between book and music hatched numerous musical changes. "There was a song called 'While These Dreams Existed' that was replaced by another song, and one called 'Mystery Girl' that was dropped. We had written a new song for Sebastian called 'That Oughta Show Her,' when Sebastian was talking to Triton about how they were going to discipline Ariel. I really loved that song, but we just didn't need a new song for Sebastian. It was a balance issue."

Composing a Broadway musical, Menken says, is all about balance. "It's a matter of working with the structure of the piece, of guarding the songs and the integrity of the song score, but at the same time being open to change. Economy is a huge part of a musical. At the same time, in my experience, if you cut a little too much you lose the purpose of having a song in the first place. Sometimes you sacrifice your precious song moment to make sure the overall show works. That the story is being told the best way possible."

In adding new material to the song score for the stage, Menken simply followed his original instincts, by increasing the pastiche mix, folding in new musical idioms. "If you look at Scuttle," says Menken, "the choice seemed very clear in terms of what was needed in the score and the color that could be added. I mean, Scuttle is clearly a vaudevillian." And "She's in Love" added a dose of girl groups from the sixties (which one can hear from the score of *Little Shop of Horrors* and is a style that's clearly dear to Menken's heart).

"When I wrote *The Little Mermaid* film, the dominant stylistic model was Disney," Menken recalls. "Howard and I were 'doing Disney.' And so, yes, the impulse came from an eclectic place, but every song moment was stylized in such a way that the musical vocabulary was clear. We had just come off *Little Shop of Horrors*, and in one corner of the universe you really can see *The Little Mermaid* as the Ashman/Menken follow up to *Little Shop*. In one case we were adapting a B movie with doo-wop music, and in the other case we were adapting Disney. And in adapting Disney, we made choices that we really wanted to feel could stand alongside anything from *Snow White* and *Cinderella* to *Peter Pan* and *Pinocchio* or *Lady and the Tramp*."

And although that might have been daunting to another composer and lyricist, Menken jokes, "We were just dumb enough to think we could pull it off." And on a more serious note, "You know, it didn't feel that daunting, thanks to Howard. He was simply the best we had. He was probably the best talent of our generation, and he didn't wear it on his sleeve. He was a temperamental, wiry, pushy, adorably wonderful, smart, loving person. And he just loved musical theater. I mean, the key to what we do is loving it first. Howard loved the form. And he loved rock and roll, and he loved American music. So when we worked in forms that he loved, that love came though.

"Now besides that, of course, from just about the first minute we were working on *The Little Mermaid*, Howard knew he had a sword dangling over his head because he was

Collaborating on a Broadway musical is, Menken says, "a matter of working with the structure of the piece, of guarding the songs and the integrity of the song score, but at the same time being open to changing things." When Francesca Zambello took over as director, says Menken, she "stood back and let the rest of us take the wheel. Then gradually she began to establish her authority. And when we reached the theater, Francesca turned into the general in the room. She put on the uniform and said, 'Okay, the buck stops here.' And we still had our discussions and our disagreements—I call them battles, but sometimes you have to battle no matter how much you like someone.

"And she would say, 'You know, darling, we have to make some cuts here,' and I would say, 'But that's essential to the song and blah, blah, blah.' Often Tom made the final decision. Doug Wright was a wonderful influence because he's such a nice man. He's smart. He avoids battles. They're not his thing. I don't have a problem with them, because I know that I get impassioned about the work.

"There are still things in the show I think Francesca would like to change that I lobbied for and fought for and will remain. There are things that I would like to see changed, but Francesca has put them in place, and I have to recognize that they work—and she's the director. That's pretty normal for any musical, that you know you have to okay things that are painful to you. It's something everyone has to do at some point in life.

sick, but the rest of us didn't know. How being ill affected the intensity of his work or the emotional content of his work, I'll never know. But there were levels in Howard that were pretty intense.

Working with Thomas Schumacher as the producer of *The Little Mermaid* for Broadway, Menken reports, has been as collaborative a process as making the original film. "Tom is very, very collaborative," says the composer. "He is able to wear the authority of producer in terms of handling all the details that we creative people don't want to know about and the creative elements in a very graceful way. His abilities as a producer are impressive."

theater dramatists to discover what are the right choices because they're there; it's not like you really invent them. Certainly, if Jerry Zacks and Julie Taymor direct the same musical, the result will be very different, but the chances are they will have faced many of the same choices. This is especially true if you're starting with a writing-driven project as we were with *The Little Mermaid*. Our choices are limited, but within those limitations we can let our creativity flow. It's the same with choreography and all the other elements: you get a chance to shine because of the limitations the form and the story and the needs of the actors and the audience impose. The real trick is to surprise people with something they already know is coming.

"After I came into the project and started evolving the script with Doug," remembers Francesca Zambello, "we had to work in the songs that Alan and Glenn had already written. And I have to say that the two of them were unusually flexible about writing new songs and rewriting them. I think it's the hardest thing for any artist to keep being told, 'Go back and do this again, reinvent this moment again, do it this way, or bring this to the table.' And they were great about all of that. They had already been working on the show for years, so they were not only flexible, they were able to turn things around very quickly."

"When you write a musical," Menken continues, "from the moment you say I'm going to adapt something—and 99.9 percent of the time you're adapting some pre-existing work—you are limiting the number of choices. Then you add everything you must have in the story structurally. Now your choices are limited again. You may think you have an infinite number of possibilities, but in my book, you start with relatively few, and you just have to discover them.

"For example, I see a moment that I know needs a song. I can write maybe fifteen strange, interesting, okay songs. Maybe I can write one great one. It's our job as musical-

"For the entire process of the show Ariel's basic arc hasn't really changed. To me what's changed, number one, is the level of adult passion that exists between Ariel and Eric. That's a big change. I think Sierra Boggess really bridges the innocent little girl-like quality of Ariel," continues Menken, who is the father of two girls who have grown into womanhood since he first wrote the *Little Mermaid* songs. In the show, you see the young teenager quality with a more three-dimensional womanly quality. If you come to the theater wanting to see the Ariel from the movie, you're going to see her. And if you come in wanting to see a more dimensional Ariel, you're going to see that."

ABOVE: Composer Alan Menken (left) and lyricist Glenn Slater go over one of their ten new songs for the musical score.

But composers alone do not, in most cases, write songs by themselves. They work with lyricists who write the words, a task that is perhaps trickier for *The Little Mermaid* than it might be for other shows because some of the songs in the score already had lyrics going into the production. Glenn Slater, the new lyricist for the Broadway production of *Little Mermaid*, had to work within the idiom established by Howard Ashman but for a different medium and a later time, all the while making all the pieces work as a seamless whole.

Glenn Slater and Alan Menken began working on the stage version of *The Little Mermaid* in 2001 (shortly after Slater won the ASCAP Foundation Richard Rodgers New Horizon Award). They were originally paired for a sequel to Disney's *Who Framed Roger Rabbit*: they had the same agent, and Slater had worked already for Disney Animation. They wrote half a dozen songs for the sequel, which was never made, but they completed *Home on the Range*, which proved to be a bonding experience for both of them.

"When I first started working with Alan," remembers Slater, "I was twenty-eight years old. I went up to his house, and I was sitting in his studio, with all of his equipment and the Oscars and the Grammys and the Golden Globes sort of gazing down at me. So here I was, working with this guy who's a giant in this field, and I was . . . 'intimidated slightly' would not be an overstatement. But the more I heard him talk about his relationship with Howard Ashman, the more I figured out that what made their songs great was that they came at things from different angles, bouncing against each other.

"I realized that my job was to challenge him, to say, 'We can do better' and have him challenge me in the same way—because Alan and I naturally approach writing songs from very different angles.

"Alan has an incredible instinct for honing in on the emotional core of the moment and capturing it in the music. My approach is more intellectual. I tend to analyze everything and try to figure out the themes and the character arcs and make everything balance and have meaning and a relationship to the whole."

So how do the Broadway/Hollywood composer and the Harvard English graduate actually work? "Generally we will sit in a room and discuss the concepts for a scene and try to come up with some way to musicalize the scene that feels fresh and original," says Slater. "Then either Alan will just sit at the piano and start trying to find the emotional core of that scene, or I will throw out a title, or a line of dialogue, and he'll work from there. It goes very piecemeal after that. Sometimes he'll write an entire piece of music in one swoop, and I'll take it home and write the words. Sometimes I will bring back to him a chunk of lyric or a full lyric, and he will work off of that, creating a piece of music, and then I'll go and fill in the blanks. It's very back and forth."

In the course of the long development of *The Little Mermaid*, that "back and forth" produced what Slater estimates to be significantly more new songs than ever made it into the finished show. "I have somewhere between twenty and thirty songs in the trunk from the show," he says with a chuckle. "Some of the songs we thought we needed turned out not to work for the script and the characters as they evolved. And sometimes we wrote several songs for the same moment before we hit the right one. We wrote three different songs for Triton to sing in the first act. There were three different songs to introduce Sebastian.

"One of the great challenges of working in the theater is that it's not about writing a great song; it's about writing a perfect song in the exact right spot."
—GLENN SLATER

"One of the great challenges of working in the theater is that it's not about writing a great song; it's about writing a perfect song in the exact right spot." Additionally, the songs from the movie fell at specific moments in the plot and couldn't be moved, but they created some difficulties in composing the songs for the stage version.

"One of the things that makes the movie so great is that Howard was trained, as many of us are, at the BMI Workshop, where you learn certain fundamentals of the structure, the formula, as it were. Alan and Howard knew how to work with those formulaic moments, the 'I want' song, for example, and to use them in ways that don't feel formulaic."

In *The Little Mermaid*, the "I want" song is "Part of Your World," and it appears almost a third of the way into the movie, way too late in the Broadway scheme of things. You can't have your leading lady not sing until half an hour into the show. But if Ariel has to sing before "Part of Your World," which would normally be the leading lady's first number, what on earth is she going to sing? So that's where 'The World Above' comes from. In the same way, Ursula's 'Poor Unfortunate Souls' is halfway into the show, but we need to know something about the villain's motives long before that, so we had a slot that eventually got filled with 'I Want the Good Times Back.'"

Still, as Slater points out, you can't waste time in a musical, you can't have a production number (not even a solo) at every plot point. Some things have to be left to the dialogue. "We had to strike a balance between exploring some of the characters and themes in more depth and keeping the story moving forward with the velocity that the film has. The film is so brilliantly put together that there's not a wasted line in it. Everything in it is a plot point, a character point, or a joke, one after the other without any letup. It's so lean!"

Yet another challenge for the lyricist was the fact that most of his audience would know the lyrics to the original Howard Ashman/Alan Menken songs by heart. "I decided early on that what I wanted was to make the new material seem as much an extension of what Howard did as possible. Howard had a very specific voice, a very specific lyric-writing voice, which I wanted to try to maintain as much as I could.

"The original songs from the movie are already classics, and nothing new would be perceived in the same light as those classics, because there's a big difference between hearing something for the first time and hearing a song you already love. So my job was not to compete with Howard; it was to support the songs that already existed and to make the new material seem to be part of a whole with the original songs at the pinnacle. That took a lot of the pressure off me.

"But, you know, I hope that when people hear a song like 'She's in Love,' the tone of it and the style of it and the way language is used and the playfulness of it are reminiscent of something

Sierra Boggess rehearses a grotto scene at the New 42nd Street Studios.

THIS PAGE: An actor's rehearsal life is never done!
TOP LEFT: Tituss Burgess and Sean Palmer. TOP RIGHT: Kay
Trinidad. CENTER: Tim Federle, Arbender J. Robinson, Robert
Creighton, Eddie Korbich. BOTTOM LEFT: Cicily Daniels.

that Howard would do. I hope that 'Her Voice' and 'If Only' have something of the timeless quality of Howard's ballads. I hope that the songs that are more book-oriented, like 'Beyond My Wildest Dreams' feel like the extensions of the existing material and not like something alien suddenly plopped in.

"My goal as a lyricist is to disappear. If you get to the end of a song that I've written and say, 'Gosh, that lyricist is clever!' I've probably failed, because you shouldn't be thinking about me; you should be completely enmeshed in the moment. And so, for me, what most people consider the hard part— the rhyming and the cleverness—is relatively easy. Ninety percent of writing the lyric is the idea. If the lyrics to 'Positoovity' are clever, I want them to reflect Scuttle's cleverness. I want it to be right for that moment in the show where

Ariel is starting a new life and needs a little boost to her self-esteem. Songs in musicals have to be much more than just songs."

In fact, the songs of *The Little Mermaid* are so well known that at several moments during the show the audience begins to applaud at the first identifiable notes of one of their favorites, and a cheer goes up at nearly every performance at the first marimba notes of "Under the Sea." The songs are so familiar that they became part of the language the producing staff used to communicate with the audience.

Music director Michael Kosarin (who is called "Koz" by his colleagues) has worked with Alan Menken for over fifteen years, since the Broadway production of *Beauty and the Beast*. He's known to the cast as "the voice of Alan Menken," and he brings the songwriter's authority to the rehearsals (he taught the songs to the cast) and the performances, most of which he conducts. One of his tasks was to write the overture for the show.

"We went through three or four different overtures," says Kosarin, who is also credited as the show's vocal arranger and composer of incidental music. "Tom Schumacher's initial thought was, 'Let's give them all the new songs, they already know the old songs. So write a big old-fashioned overture like one of the classic overtures from the '50s, like *Gypsy*.' So I wrote that, and it was a lot of fun. You can hear a little of it now in the exit music," he laughs.

"Little by little we started morphing into what we have now, which is kind of a 'greatest hits.' Everyone wants to hear what they know from the movie, so the final version of the overture kind of reassures them. It says, 'Okay, sit back, you're in the right place. You're in the right seat. This is the music that you've come to hear.'"

But adapting a film score for a show is much more than a matter of re-playing the original—or even of resetting it for a pit orchestra of seventeen instead of a studio orchestra of fifty or sixty, which is typical of animated film production. "Danny Troob," says Kosarin of the show's orchestrator (who has worked on many Disney film and theater projects as well as on the Broadway version of *Little Shop of Horrors* and

other shows), "is a genius of an orchestrator. He completely reconceived a lot of the sounds so that they're hotter or more suited to theater. And that redefines the sound. At the same time, he knew that we couldn't be too far off from what people were used to hearing in the film."

Sometimes the audience hears something familiar in a very different way. The melody of "One Step Closer," for example, comes from the theme Menken wrote for the underscore of the *Mermaid* film. Each of the film characters, in fact, has a musical theme, which Menken drew on for the new material in the show. The melody for "One Step Closer," which Eric sings to Ariel in the second act as a sign of his growing love, comes from Eric's musical motif in Menken's film score.

All of which is part of keeping the score organic despite the numerous differences between the film and the show. "Sometimes people in the cast would come to me and say, 'I forget now, did Howard Ashman write that or did Glenn write it? Was that in the movie? I think it's in the movie.' That happened more than once."

Standing at the center of all the development, all the changes, elisions, and expansions, of course, was the show's director, Francesca Zambello, who right from the start found her material compelling but knew she needed to shift the emphasis of the story to something newer than the film and to anchor the show to Ariel's progression from girl to woman, from daughter to individual in her own right.

TOP: Music director Michael Kosarin (left) and orchestrator Danny Troob, two of Disney's most esteemed longtime collaborators.
LEFT: Kosarin, known as "Koz," conducts the cast-album recording.

"I had to look at this project through three separate lenses," explains the director. "First, there's the lens of the original story: what did "The Little Mermaid" mean to Hans Christian Andersen in 1836. Then, there's the lens of the film and what was going on around the creation of the film in the early 1980s. What did the story of the little mermaid mean to Howard Ashman in the early years of the AIDS epidemic, to a man who was himself infected by the virus?

"Then, most importantly," Zambello continues, "how do we look at the story today, twenty years after the film was written? To me, that involves the rise of girl power. It involves questions of diversity, which is why the show is cast the way it is, with people of different sizes and shapes and colors. At the end of the show when Triton embraces Eric and the two worlds become one, the show sends a message of tolerance, which I think is an important one for today. So the big three thematic things for me were tolerance, diversity, and girl power."

Ironically, then, perhaps, since she's the most important character in the show, Ariel was among the last to be cast. "I think it's always the way in musicals," Zambello suggests. "You never seem to be able to find the ingenue couple. I think that's because everybody thinks they know what the ingenue couple should be, because everybody has a different perception of their own youth, and what first love is, and those are the things that are key in those characters.

"It's difficult to find the perfect match for several reasons, not the least of which, for this show, is that both the young male and the young female lead have to act and dance as well as sing. They have to have chemistry together. They have to look and sound good together. When the girl gets the prince at the end of the show, you have to be cheering for them, and we needed to imagine how this Eric and this Ariel would handle the changes in their characters that we were planning to make in the story.

"I mean, from the beginning, Tom, Doug, Alan, and I wanted to give Eric some more gravitas, for want of a better word. We wanted to make him more interesting, to create a dilemma and a dramatic arc for him as well as for her—which is that he has to get married and can't find a woman he wants to marry. And this was especially important since we were taking away from him the swashbuckling rescue of Ariel from the clutches of Ursula at the end. We wanted to give Eric a ballad in act one, a number to parallel Ariel's 'Part of Your World,' which is where 'Her Voice' comes from. And Alan and Glenn did a great job on that song, because the voice is what connects the characters. Ariel's voice and what it means is at the center of *The Little Mermaid*."

Sierra Boggess and Sean Palmer rehearse "One Step Closer."

The Songs

Fathoms Below

Music by Alan Menken—Lyrics by Howard Ashman & Glenn Slater

I'll tell you a tale of the bottomless blue

An' it's hey to the starboard, heave ho!

Brave sailor, beware, 'cause a big 'uns a-brewin'

Mysterious fathoms below!

Daughters of Triton

Music by Alan Menken—Lyrics by Howard Ashman

In concert we hope to enlighten
The hearts of the merfolk with music's swell. . . .
And then there is the youngest
In her musical debut
Our seventh little sister
We're presenting her to you. . . .

Sierra Boggess

The World Above

Music by Alan Menken—Lyrics by Glenn Slater

This is where I belong
Beneath the clear blue here!
I feel completely new here
In the world above!

Human Stuff

Music by Alan Menken—Lyrics by Glenn Slater

Sierra Boggess, Eddie Korbich, Cody Hanford

Pick up the dingelhopper, just like so
Twirl it the way I'm twirling now!
Give it a little yank, and there ya go!
You're what they call the "dog's meow!"

I Want the Good Times Back

Music by Alan Menken—Lyrics by Glenn Slater

Tyler Maynard, Sherie Rene Scott, Derrick Baskin

I want the good times back!
I want those grand ol' days!
I want the twisted nights
The sick delights
The wild soireés!

Part of Your World

Music by Alan Menken—Lyrics by Howard Ashman

Sierra Boggess

I've got gadgets and gizmos a-plenty

I've got who's-its and what's-its galore

You want thing-a-mabobs? I've got twenty

But who cares? No big deal

I want more. . . .

She's in Love

Music by Alan Menken—Lyrics by Glenn Slater

She's dizzy and she's dreamy
Her head's up in the foam
Her eyes have gone all gleamy
It's like there's no one home

Sean Palmer

Her Voice

Music by Alan Menken—Lyrics by Glenn Slater

Somewhere there's a girl
 Who's like a swell of endless music
Somewhere she is singing
 And her song is meant for me

Under the Sea

Music by Alan Menken—Lyrics by Howard Ashman

Just look at the world around you
Right here on the ocean floor
Such wonderful things surround you
What more is you lookin' for?

Tyler Maynard, Sierra Boggess, Derrick Baskin

Sweet Child

Music by Alan Menken—Lyrics by Glenn Slater

Who will ease her woes and worries?
Who will help her get her man?
Sweet child,
Perhaps the Sea Witch can.

Poor Unfortunate Souls

Music by Alan Menken—Lyrics by Howard Ashman

Sierra Boggess, Sherie Rene Scott, Tyler Maynard

Come on, you poor unfortunate soul
Go ahead—make your choice!
I'm a very busy woman
And I haven't got all day
It won't cost you much
Just your voice!

Positoovity

Music by Alan Menken—Lyrics by Glenn Slater

So stand right up and dust your seat
And walk real tall upon your own two feet
And sure, you'll trip and make mistakes
But you got what it takes!

Beyond My Wildest Dreams

Music by Alan Menken—Lyrics by Glenn Slater

Sierra Boggess

I'd hoped and wished
And wondered what I'd do here
Wished and prayed
And pictured what I'd see
Prayed and wow!
My prayers are coming true here!
Look at it all, look how it gleams!
Lovely beyond my wildest dreams . . .

Les Poissons

Music by Alan Menken — Lyrics by Howard Ashman

And now for the grand finale
La pièce de résistance
A delicacy, by golly
You won't find in restaurants!

Sierra Boggess and Sean Palmer

One Step Closer

Music by Alan Menken—Lyrics by Glenn Slater

Dancing is a language that is felt instead of heard
But it says much more than language ever could
And ev'ry little step
Ev'ry single step
Is one step closer . . .
To being understood

Kiss the Girl

Music by Alan Menken—Lyrics by Howard Ashman

There you see her
Sitting there across the way
She don't got a lot to say
But there's something about her
And you don't know why
But you're dying to try
You wanna kiss the girl

Sierra Boggess, Seal Palmer, Tituss Burg

Sean Palmer and Sierra Boggess

If Only

Music by Alan Menken—Lyrics by Glenn Slater

If only you could know
The things I long to say
If only I could tell you
What I wish I could convey

It's in my ev'ry glance
My heart's an open book
You'd see it all at once
If only you would look

The Contest

Music by Alan Menken • Lyrics by Glenn Slater

Welcome, dear friends, to our contest—
The first that this kingdom has ever seen!
We gather today for a vocal display
So our prince may at last choose a queen!

Finale

Music by Alan Menken   Lyrics by Howard Ashman & Glenn Slater

Sean Palmer and Sierra Boggess

And now at last
Love has surpassed
Each tribulation!
Mermaid and man
Finally can
Join and be one!

School of Fish

"I'M SUCH A GUPPY," sighs Flounder whenever he finds his courage waning. He'd rather be a shark, but he's got some growing up to do. *The Little Mermaid* employs two Flounders and splits the performances between them (that way the role is always covered if one boy is sick or on vacation). The kids have plenty of courage, but because they are minors, special rules govern their appearances. For one thing, they have to attend school for a proscribed number of hours each day during the rehearsal and tech periods. For *The Little Mermaid*, the boys' tutor was Serena Stanley from On Location Education.

Children in theater are always accompanied by a chaperone, who is informally called a "kid wrangler." For this production, it was John Mara. He keeps the youngsters out of trouble and out of harm's way, makes sure they get from their fourth-floor dressing room to their stage entrances on time, and keeps an eye out for safety issues, such as flying scenery. The chaperone might help his charges memorize and rehearse their lines and might also pass on the finer points of backstage etiquette.

Child actors have a notoriously short run in most roles because they grow out of them so quickly. For *The Little Mermaid*, the two boys originally cast as Flounder, J.J. Singleton and Cody Hanford, spent nearly a year rehearsing and doing the out-of-town trial shows in Denver, but they had outgrown the part before opening night in New York. By the premiere on January 10, they had moved on to other jobs and been replaced in *Mermaid* by Trevor Braun and Brian D'Addario.

TOP: Chaperone John Mara with J.J. Singleton (middle) and Cody Hanford at a New York rehearsal. ABOVE: BFs ("Boy Flounders") Brian D'Addario (left) and Trevor Braun at the Lunt-Fontanne Theatre.

CLOCKWISE FROM LEFT: John Mara with Cody in rehearsal; Mara with Trevor and Brian in their Broadway dressing room; Cody and J.J. rehearse "She's in Love" with the mersisters (including Kay Trinidad).

101

ARIEL'S

part four

WORLD

THE ANCIENT GREEKS, WHO invented theater as we know it, had almost no scenic flexibility whatever in their stone amphitheaters. Still, Aristotle thought that spectacle played an essential role in the telling of dramatic stories. For the Greeks, "spectacle"—the elements that the audience saw and heard in the theater—had more to do with dance, staging, and costumes (including masks), which are certainly part of what we mean today when we speak of a show's visual production. But there are many more resources these days than the Greeks ever dreamed of for their outdoor performances under the afternoon sun.

Complex stage pictures are now typical of large-scale Broadway productions, and visual stage artists can create just about anything the imagination can conjure—from flying cars or crashing chandeliers to a rotating Pride Rock, a beast who transforms into a prince, or a perfectly proper English nanny who can sail over the heads of the audience on an umbrella.

To create the physical world of *The Little Mermaid*, director Francesca Zambello nominated a frequent colleague of hers, theater designer George Tsypin, who was born in Kazakhstan in 1954 (when it was part of the Soviet Union), but who has been a resident of the United States since 1979. His opera credentials include designs for the Salzburg Festival, the Opera de la Bastille in Paris, Covent Garden, La Scala, and the Metropolitan Opera, where his Kirov production of *War and Peace* has recently been performed. Among the other forward-thinking directors with whom he has been associated are Peter Sellars, Julie Taymor (who directed

Disney's *The Lion King* on Broadway), Andrei Konchalovsky, and Robert Falls (director of *Elton John and Tim Rice's AIDA* for Disney).

But the very highly cultured, Russian-educated architect is also fully acquainted with the Broadway stage. After receiving a master of fine arts degree in theater from New York University, Tsypin went to work for legendary Broadway designer David Mitchell, serving an apprenticeship on such popular musical and nonmusical fare as *La Cage aux Folles* and *Biloxi Blues*. He was thoroughly versed in theater design before focusing on opera, and one of his most meaningful collaborations with Zambello was a production of *West Side Story* on a huge abstract set built over a lake in Austria.

What made the designer seem perfect to Zambello for *The Little Mermaid* were Tsypin's previous explorations in transparency and translucency. "I knew that George would understand how to do an underwater set," recalls Zambello. "It would be very sculptural, using a lot of glass and light." Tsypin, she knew, liked to engage an audience's imagination, bringing it only so far and expecting them to fill in the rest.

Although they had not met, producer Thomas Schumacher knew of Tsypin's work. It was Schumacher who hired Julie Taymor to direct *The Lion King* on Broadway, and Tsypin had designed the *Magic Flute* that Taymor directed at the Met, which Schumacher had seen.

The first "audition" model that Tsypin created still exists; it shows four essentially vertical, stage-high abstract architectural elements made of a plastic material that resembles glass. Described as everything from reinvented chess pieces to mechanical bottle openers, they are altogether modern, yet they maintain something of the personality of history, too: they are artifacts of some lost world—Atlantis, perhaps—intended to move, transform, and interact. Additional more specific set pieces, like Ariel's secret grotto for "human stuff" and Scuttle's outcropping of rock, would augment the four elaborate stage "towers."

OPPOSITE AND ABOVE: Inspired by marine life, George Tsypin created these two development models depicting an underwater scene, in cool blues, and one on land, in bright oranges.

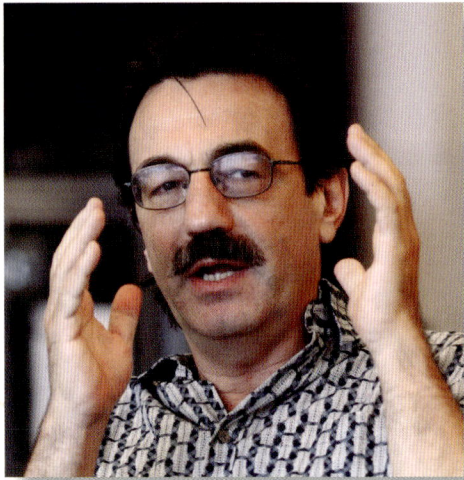

"We wanted to create a sensibility of the underwater world that would spark the imagination."

—GEORGE TSYPIN

Tsypin's enormous design studio looks a lot like a science lab, and he is admittedly interested in many worlds. He doesn't just design in this space, he also builds, and many of the prototype pieces for *The Little Mermaid* were fabricated by Tsypin and his staff of like-minded souls. There is something of the latter-day Renaissance man about Tsypin.

What does he think drew the interest of Zambello and Schumacher in him for *The Little Mermaid*? "I don't know exactly," he says, conceding that for his own part he was, as always, interested in stretching himself to do things he'd never done before. "I think one reason that they asked me," he supposes, "is that for twenty-five years I've been developing this whole technique of using transparent materials. And even though I've never gone as far as we did on this show, I guess it felt like the right way to approach the material.

"The essential visual metaphor for *The Little Mermaid*," he continues, "is water. All of my work has been getting more and more fluid, and I've been exploring organic shapes that maybe look like something that could be under the sea." They were also designed to take light, to reflect, and to glow, so the lighting design would give the stage design its full presence; the two would go hand-in-hand."

Another fundamental aspect of the set is the strict difference Tsypin envisioned between the underwater world of the merfolk and the world above, the world inhabited by the footed creatures like Prince Eric and Grimsby. The underwater world, as Tsypin saw it, would always be represented by the color blue, the world above would be yellow. The set pieces would be designed to be used in both above-water and below-water scenes, leaving lighting designer Natasha Katz a great deal of creative leeway.

"You know, we're not trying to illustrate every plant in the sea," Tsypin says. "We wanted to create a sensibility of the underwater world that would spark the imagination. Every detail of the set is inspired by something real but transformed and interpreted to make it part of the fantastical world of *The Little Mermaid*."

BELOW: A late model for Ariel's grotto, in which transparency and translucency are the key design concepts.
OPPOSITE: A model of the grotto festooned with Ariel's collection of "human stuff" (INSET) and the final set piece for the production (Sierra Boggess as Ariel).

One of the inspirations for the set was a famous painting now at the Museo Nacional del Prado in Madrid called *The Garden of Earthly Delights* by Hieronymus Bosch—not for its motivating religious or allegorical content but for its fantastical architectural structures. There is a pink towerlike building in the left panel of the Bosch triptych, which was painted from 1503 to 1504, that influenced the stage design quite specifically. "Certainly, not everyone in the audience is going to understand this point of reference," Tsypin says, but it taught me the lesson of how to stylize and create a world of our own.

"So I tried to come up with shapes that were versatile enough to speak to the story and to the metaphors of the story and to the magic of the theater. And maybe we're challenging the audience in a way, but most people underestimate the audience. Audiences are quite able to follow an imaginative lead to all kinds of places.

"If you have a person onstage wearing a tail representing a fish, your imagination is already engaged, because that is not a fish. It's an actor in a costume. If you invite the audience to a game of imagination, they will play with you. A lot is left for the audience to figure out, because that's part of the joy. So you look at a man in a red suit and you think, 'Oh, he's a crab.' But he's not a crab, he's a person playing a role. In the animated film you have animals that look a little like people; in the show you have people who look a little bit like animals.

[continued on page 116]

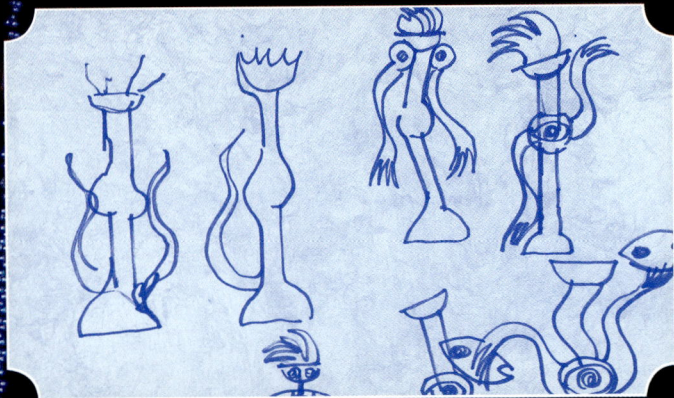

Detail of a page of Tsypin's early "doodles," as he calls them, showing ideas for the two main columns that are signature elements of the show's set design.

Every piece of dozens of development models were sculpted, molded, and cast—an enormously time-consuming process.

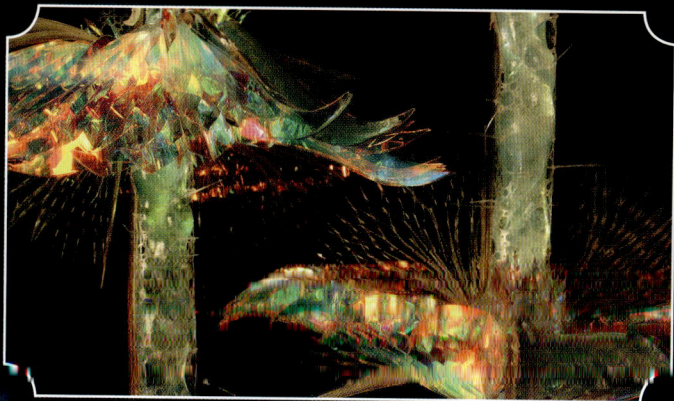

A model of the two main set columns shows the relationship of their fans when they are opened, as for "Under the Sea."

One of the meticulously detailed models for "Under the Sea," showing the two columns (which were reversed in the staging.)

The set going up in Denver. OPPOSITE INSET: A model of the capital from one of the columns with Tsypin's signature organic design. ABOVE INSET: A model of the fan for one of the columns shows the way it stretches open like a paper accordion.

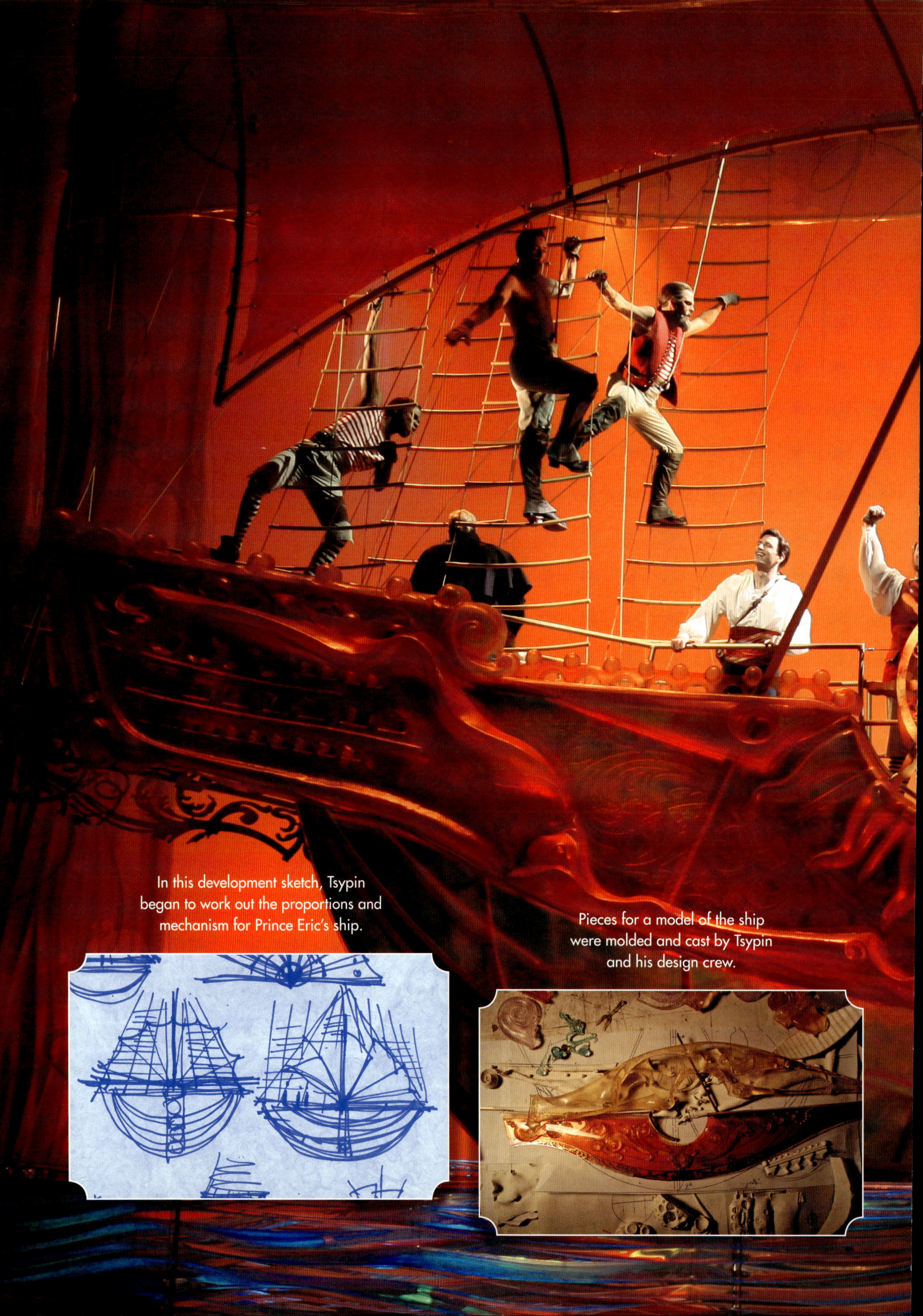

In this development sketch, Tsypin began to work out the proportions and mechanism for Prince Eric's ship.

Pieces for a model of the ship were molded and cast by Tsypin and his design crew.

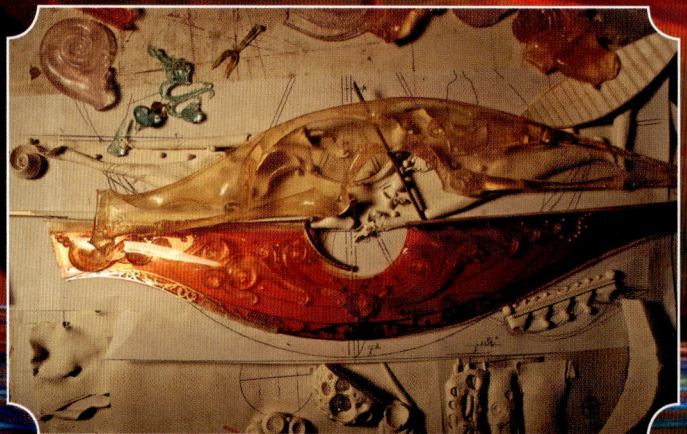

A full stage model for the ship in one of its many guises. Every element of the set design went through dozens of refinements between idea and finished piece.

This model shows how pieces of the ship swing apart like giant pendulums for the storm scene.

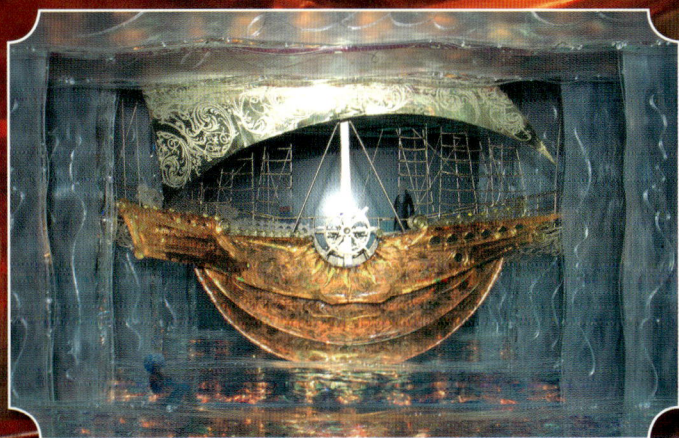

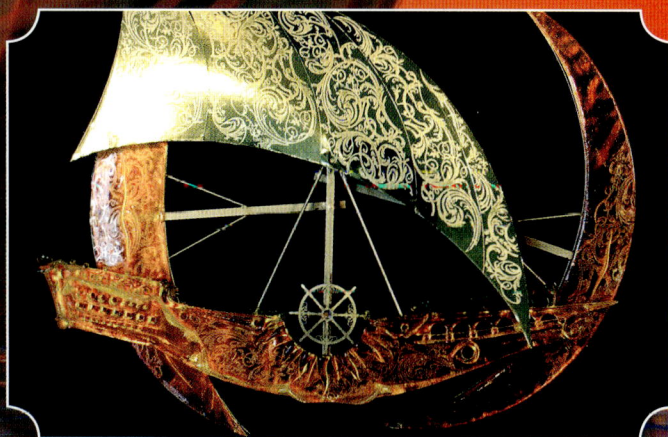

THESE PAGES: Prince Eric's ship hangs backstage, surrounded by lighting instruments. INSET: A model of the ship's rigging.

2402

INSET: A computer-generated scale drawing of the metal plating for the ship, which is used as a template for the set builder to lay out the basic shapes.

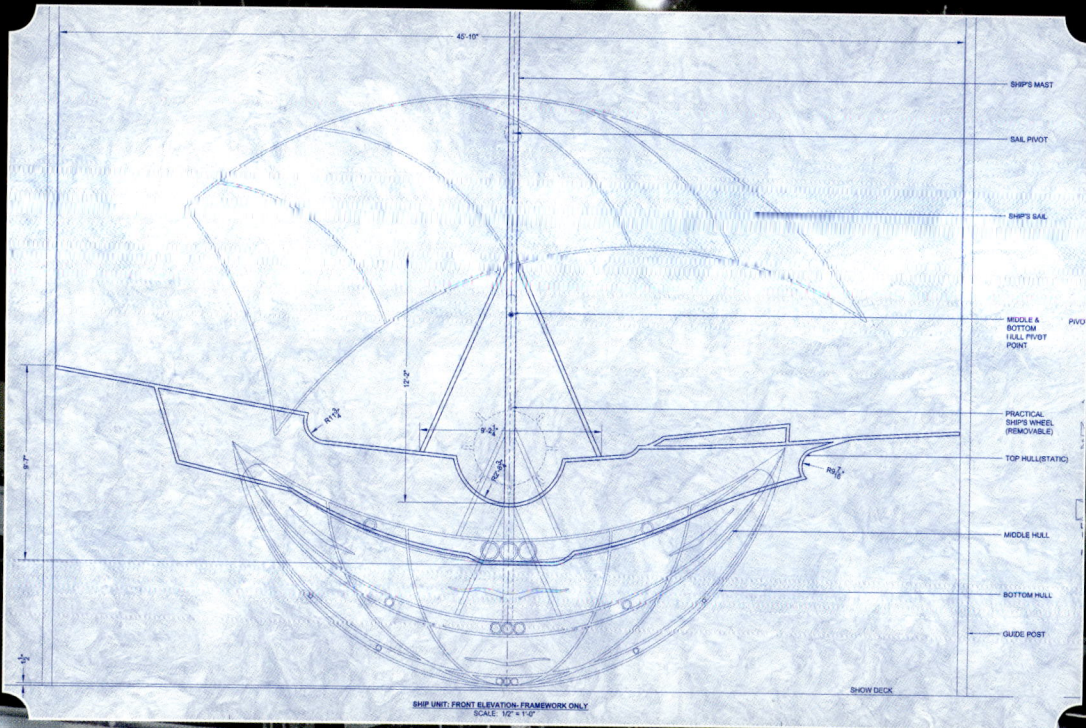

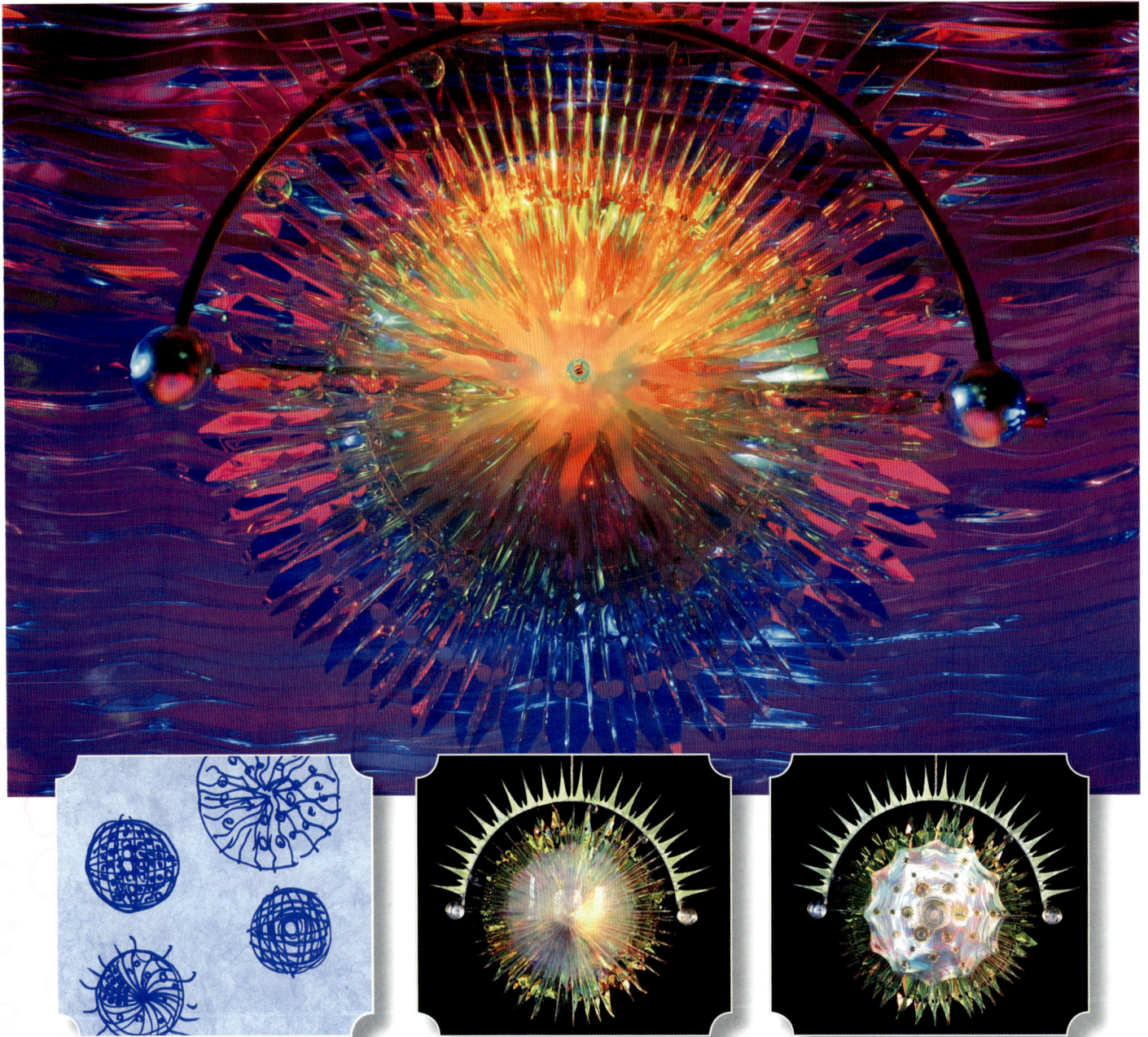

TOP: The "sun" from the final scene. ABOVE, FROM LEFT: Detail of a sketch and models for the two versions of the set piece—one for above water and one for below. OPPOSITE: King Triton, standing before the "underwater" sun.

"The same is true of the set. I can't put a real plant or a real coral reef next to a person representing a fish. The whole visualization of the show has to become part of a similar world that we create for the audience to enjoy, to participate in by filling in the blank spaces for themselves."

Into every creative world, however, reality intrudes. So the challenges to creating any set design involve not only the manipulation of perception in the aesthetic realm, but also the very present here-and-now universe of physics, of gravity, of "no two objects may occupy the same space at the same time."

The stage at the Lunt-Fontanne Theatre, which was built in 1910, is small. "It's hard for the audience to imagine it while they're watching the show," says Tsypin, but what you see is just about all the space there is. "There are maybe three feet stage left and a little more stage right, but essentially, that's it."

In fact, the backstage area is so tight that the cast cannot watch the show from the wings because the wings are often full of scenery. Space at the Lunt-Fontanne is precious these days, and it's reserved for quick changes. The hallways are

Bret Shuford, Norm Lewis, and Alan Mingo, Jr.

full of props and costumes; even the stage bathroom has large pieces of the show stored in it. There are areas on the backstage floor marked as off-limits because the set needs that space. And so, the four towers of George Tsypin's original set concept eventually became two.

To conserve square footage, "I did a lot of research on how to make things collapse," Tsypin says, "and how to make something that takes very little space expand to fill the stage." That's when he came across elaborate Chinese folded-paper puzzles. Scouring New York City's Chinatown for every example he could find, Tsypin was inspired to create the expanding-collapsing hanging piece that represents the sun or a chandelier and manages to be a compelling visual element all its own. Ursula's tentacles also stretch and retract. And the "waves" of the back wall of the set, which is made of flexible plastics, opens and closes like a venetian blind and fits into an eighteen-inch slot in the floor when not unfurled.

All of this transformative machinery is complex even without the computerization of the set "towers," which move and communicate with each other by wireless command. "I mean, an audience may not know anything about the intricacies of creating theater, but they understand when something appears out of nothing. They understand stage magic, even if it only exists because I didn't have enough backstage space to store the scenery. That's one of the ways you are forced to create by limitations. And having the tentacles expand and contract

actually gives them more of a sense of being underwater."

Among the important visual elements to the entire creative team of *The Little Mermaid* was that of luminescence, of iridescence. Tsypin decided to build as much of that luster into the set as possible given the limitations of materials and safety: "Obviously there is no glass onstage," he says, "so you have to create that out of different materials. I started with the idea of something real, of bioluminescence—undersea life that has its own light source, like fireflies on land—and the notion of iridescence, like the scales from a mermaid's tail.

"That gives you something very rainbowlike and magical. So you search for materials that will look like what you want, and you try to make them behave the way you want, and then, just when you think everything is resolved, you have to address fireproofing. That was another stage we went through, and some materials had to be exchanged for other things."

LEFT AND ABOVE: Designer George Tsypin demonstrates his idea for the pods, in which actors ride, situated at the ends of the arms of the set columns. OPPOSITE: The pods in action during the Denver tryout of "Kiss the Girl."

Among the materials that did not have to be exchanged was a thin plastic sheeting, almost a film, that Tsypin discovered at Material ConneXion, a reference "library" of some 3,500 modern building materials and a well-known resource for the international design community. The film, produced by 3M, is largely transparent, but it has an opalescent sheen to it and an altogether unique way of reflecting light."

"The material is called Radiant Light Film," instructs Peter Eastman, Tsypin's associate scenic designer on *The Little Mermaid*. In fact, he points out, the designers selected two different films from the Radiant Light range because of their subtle color differences. The collapsing wave wall at the back of the set is made of what are essentially layers of PVC

(polyvinyl chloride)—a material common in building and construction—and this superpowered reflecting 3M film. "It creates such intense colors," Tsypin says, "but that's part of the beauty of underwater life, the amazing colors, the unbelievable light."

Tsypin's design raised another big issue, and that was what the lighting designer would make of a set that was part transparent and part highly reflective in unexpected ways. "Natasha was a little bit concerned," says Tsypin with a sly smile.

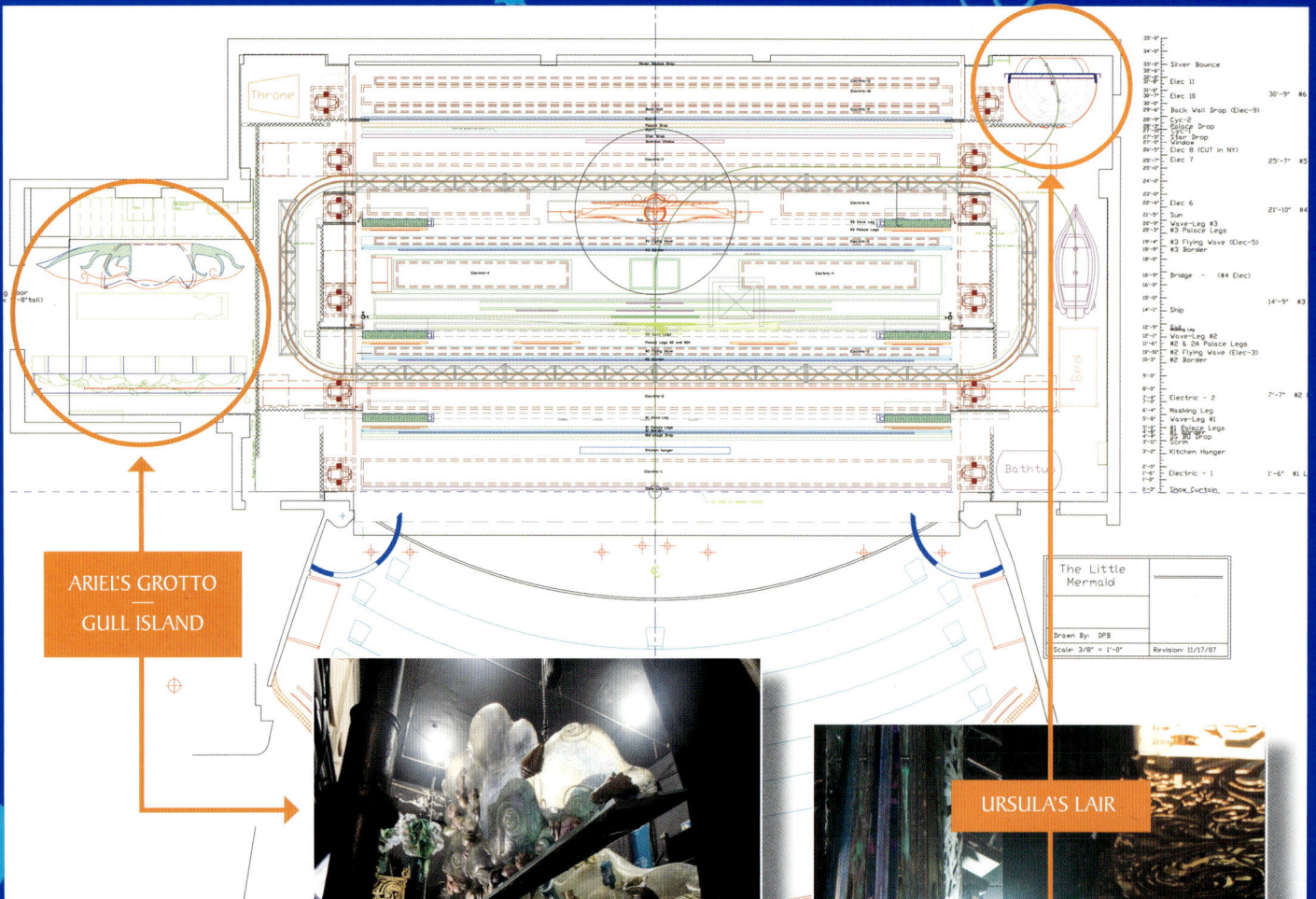

The Little Mermaid

Drawn By: DPB
Scale: 3/8" = 1'-0"   Revision: 11/17/07

ARIEL'S GROTTO — GULL ISLAND

URSULA'S LAIR

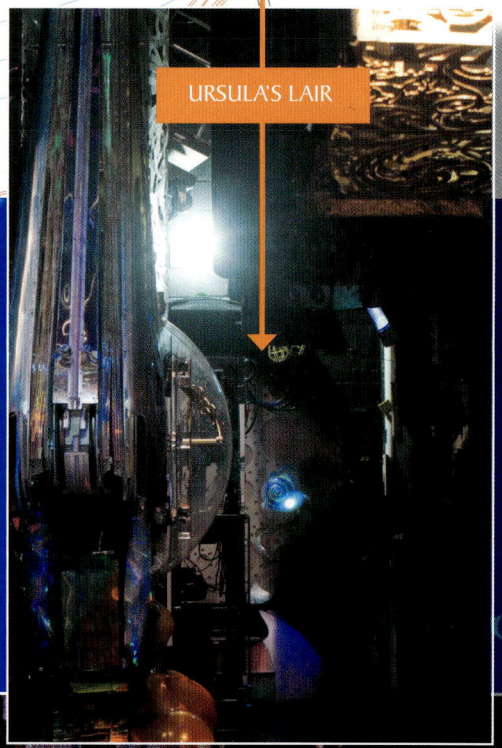

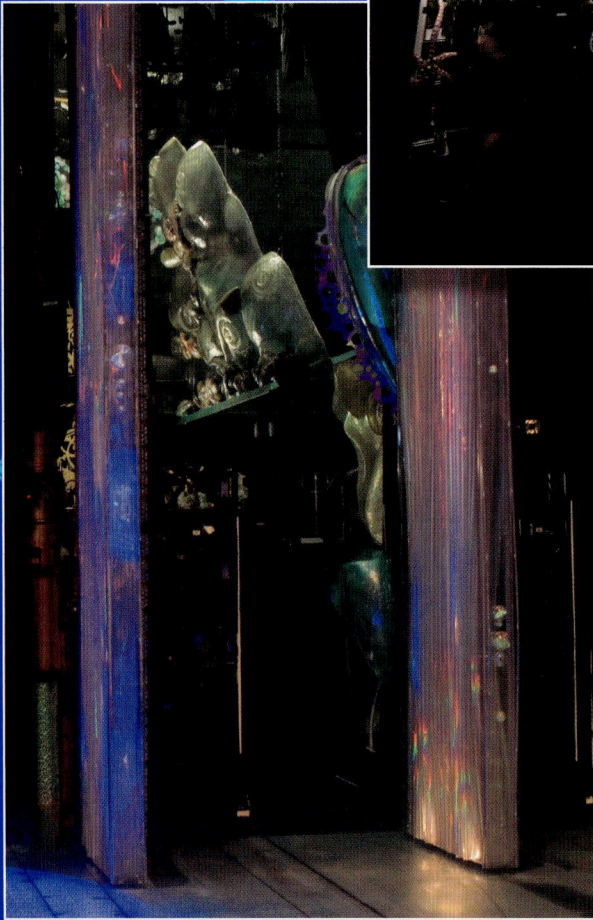

A Peek Backstage

"THERE'S NO MORE ROOM," the Mad Hatter tells Alice, although she can see that there's plenty. Unfortunately, the opposite is true in many of the older Broadway theaters, most of which were built when real estate in the neighborhood was expensive, and stage sets were mostly paintings on canvas. The luxurious auditorium of the Lunt-Fontanne may have 1,500 seats, but the actors backstage sometimes haven't got enough room to take a deep breath.

The Lunt-Fontanne opened in 1910 as The Globe. Fred Astaire danced here and Fanny Brice sang. *No, No, Nanette* opened here in 1925. In 1932, The Globe became a movie house, but it was restored in 1958 and named for husband-and-wife Broadway stars Alfred Lunt and Lynn Fontanne. It

ABOVE: Costumes and other wardrobe and makeup related items crowd a corridor just off stage left where quick changes and repairs occur.

hosted such theatrical productions as *The Sound of Music*. It was also home to Disney's *Beauty and the Beast* for nine years, and for forty-eight performances to Howard Ashman and Marvin Hamlisch's *Smile*, in which Jodi Benson introduced a song called "Disneyland."

Every inch of backstage space is used for *The Little Mermaid*. Props hang on the wall, pouf skirts and fragile fishtails hang in a corridor along the uptown side of the building. The little bathroom off the stage-door entrance doubles as a costume closet (it's where the sea horses live). Backstage space is so tight that there are "no-actor zones," and entrances have to be timed among the movements of lighting bridges and scenic elements. And many offstage crosses happen downstairs, under the stage, because there just isn't any room behind the set.

OPPOSITE: A scale drawing (top) shows the stage plan for *The Little Mermaid*, including the storage locations of many of the set pieces, some of which can be seen in the photographs of the offstage wings.

LIGHTING DESIGNER NATASHA KATZ is known as one of Broadway's brightest lights (pun intended). She graduated from Oberlin College in 1981 and since 1983 has designed some fifty Broadway productions, both musical and nonmusical. She's won two Tony Awards, for Disney's *Elton John and Tim Rice's AIDA* (2000) and Lincoln Center's *The Coast of Utopia* (2007). She has been nominated five additional times, for three Disney shows—*Beauty and the Beast*, *Tarzan*, and *The Little Mermaid*—as well as *Sweet Smell of Success* and Shakespeare's *Twelfth Night*.

Katz's impressive resume for lighting dance has included stints at the New York City Ballet, the Royal Ballet, and the American Ballet Theatre. She's done concert lighting for such headliners as Shirley MacLaine, Ann-Margret, and Tommy Tune. She's even done lighting for Niketown stores in London and New York and the Big Bang installation at the American Museum of Natural History.

Still, *The Little Mermaid* presented new challenges. Katz was brought on to the project by director Francesca Zambello. The women had worked together previously on *Cyrano de Bergerac* at the Metropolitan Opera, but Katz did not know George Tsypin. "Francesca took me out to George's studio," says Katz, "to find out if George and I would work well together. Because on a musical this size, the designers spend a lot of time together, so if it didn't look like we were a good personal match, the art would never be good. And then I walked into George's studio.

"It was nighttime," Katz remembers, "and he had about twenty models of the show all set out, and it was all translucent glass—this was before he had gotten to the pragmatic side of it where you need all the machinery under the glass—and it was so unbelievably beautiful. I wanted to work on the show right from the beginning."

Having hit it off right from the gate, the director and the designers immediately got to work on some of the strategies for the design. "Francesca and George felt that the vocabulary of color was really going to help us through the story-

> "I had to completely readapt, as if I'd never seen color before. Because nothing took light the way I expected it to."
> —NATASHA KATZ

telling," which is to say that we would limit the vocabulary. When you're underwater, it's blue. When you're above the water, it's orange or yellow. And when you're with Ursula it's kind of a danky green. We thought she might be purple at one point but decided against it. Now that's not to say there aren't variations in all of this, but ultimately, to define those three places where the story takes place, that's one of the basics of how we did it.

"There are other techniques, too, of course. When you're underwater the lighting does this kind of watery reflection effect, and I use water gobos." Gobos are a kind of stencil that fits in front of lighting instruments; gobos can be stationary or can be rotated at various speeds to provide a sense of movement. "And then there's the wave wall at the back, which is always up when you're underwater and down when you're on land. In Ursula's lair, of course, there's hardly any light at all, so it's kind of dark and gritty. And green."

In addition to aesthetic concerns and artistic tactics of the design, there are nuts and bolts to contend with. "Once you decide on basic design concepts," Katz says, "you have to deal with the really hard part. That's where you roll up your

ABOVE: Lighting designer Natasha Katz. Her primary challenge was lighting a set made of transparent materials.

sleeves, and everybody tries to figure out the real estate: where does the scenery go, where do the lights go? Because Broadway theaters are small, certainly compared to the opera houses that George and Francesca have spent a lot of their lives in. Broadway theaters are twenty-eight, twenty-nine-feet deep, so we have to collectively figure out where things will go—onstage and offstage." By comparison, the stage at the Met has 60-by-60-foot stage wagons that can roll offstage in any direction or drop below the stage level on industrial-strength elevators.

And then there was the matter of the magical new Radiant Light Film from 3M. "We did a number of mock-ups—a wave, the back wall—because how the lighting looks to the audience depends on exactly how it hits the scenery. And the

daunting aspect of the 3M material is that if you're sitting in one seat in the theater it looks different from when you're sitting in another seat." So apportioning the available space was trickier than usual, because where the lights went was more critical than usual.

"I thought it was very magnanimous of George to conceive of a set where the scenery and lighting were so completely connected," says Katz. "For this show, which has a very large lighting scheme, there are lots of lights that are there only to light the scenery. Normally, lights do double duty; they light the scenery and they light the actors. But this set was designed so that it didn't really come to life unless it

THESE PAGES: Multiple Tony Award–winning Natasha Katz managed to run the full spectrum of color on the upstage "wave" curtain.

was lit. So there are two lighting schemes, the people one and the scenery one.

"The Radiant Light material looks great with light on it, but you're never really sure what it's going to do. The way it accepts light is very intense. It's like a prism, only it's a trillion minuscule prisms, breaking down whatever light you shine on it. At one point we were even worried about glare and whether it would be difficult for the audience, but that didn't seem to be an issue once we got into the theater.

"Still," Katz continues, "I had to completely readapt, as if I'd never seen color before. Because nothing took light the way I expected it to. All of a sudden your whole understanding about what light does shifts, because of what is reflecting off of this gorgeous plastic. So I had to develop a whole new vocabulary of color.

"I have to say that this job was exciting to me right from the beginning, even though I had no idea how it was going to work. There are so many planes of scenery, which became planes of color: there's the backdrop, the legs, the actors, the waves. The feeling of vibrant colors comes from the addition of complementary colors to the basic color of any scene. So yellow helps purple really pop, for example. And *The Little Mermaid* is a fantasy, so you don't really have to be imitating nature all the time. When we finally let go in terms of the lighting, we were like kids. Kids don't know that the sky has to be blue until we tell them. For them it can be red or yellow or pink. So the more we got into it, and the more we solved the technical concerns, the more fun we were able to have."

TO THE SET AND LIGHTING design, the production team added another visual design layer in the person of Sven Ortel, the show's projection and video designer. Ortel, who was born in Germany, works primarily in England, where he has contributed to some twenty productions for the National Theatre. On Broadway he's worked on *Deuce, Faith Healer, Jumpers,* and Andrew Lloyd Weber's *The Woman in White.* He was brought on to *Mermaid* by Francesca Zambello, with whom he had worked in Vienna on a musical version of Daphne du Maurier's *Rebecca.*

Ortel's main focus on *The Little Mermaid* was to augment the underwater-ness of the set with a series of abstract, computer-generated animated sequences that add a sense of movement and light and give the stage the look of an organic universe of living things. They also help differentiate one locale from another.

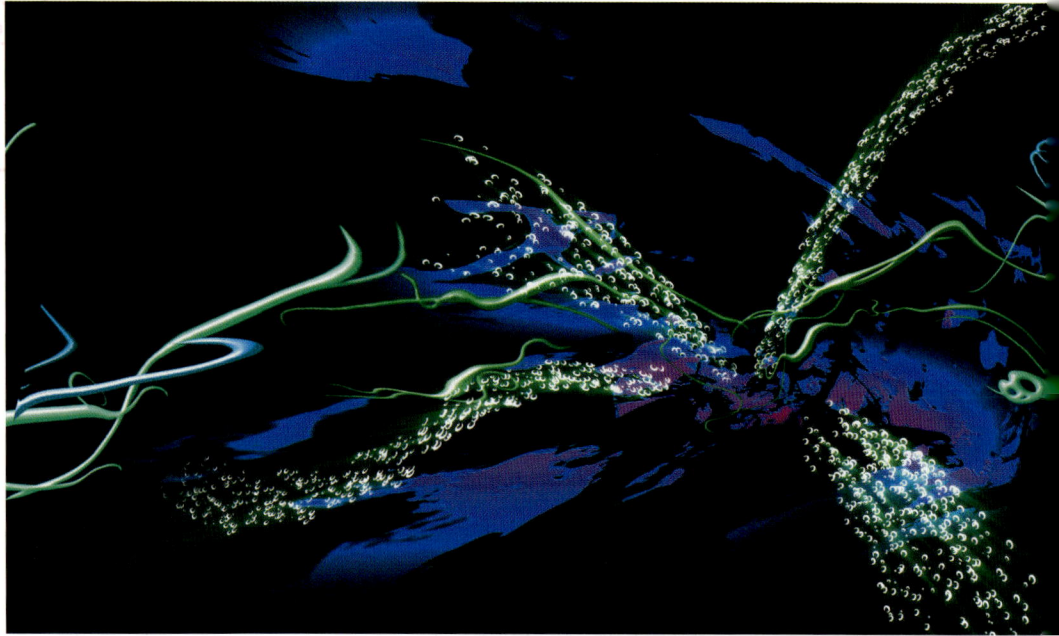

ABOVE: Sven Ortel (seated) created the video and animation effects (with programmer Peter Acken). "Freeze-frame" captures from Ortel's visual track for Ursula's demise (TOP), "She's in Love" (OPPOSITE TOP), and Ursula's lair (OPPOSITE BOTTOM).

His greatest hurdle? "Well, the brief was simple: I was told that I should create texture and density and water movement on a surface that I can't project on. That was the first thing to come to terms with. I mean a purist projection designer would say, 'No, we can't do that. Turn off the lights and give me a screen.' This is not animation like *Finding Nemo* with little fish swimming by. It's more like a pop-music video kind of approach to imagery.

"The animation augments the light because it's more flexible than traditional stage lighting. "If something needs to go from left to right and sort of sparkle, I'll just make that and project it in the right place. It's not quite the same if you have fixed tools that can only point in one direction." In fact, the speed of the animation is one of its handiest variables: the same animation might work equally well for a slight shimmer of light underwater or the livelier action of light on the surface of the sea.

At technical rehearsals, when all the designs came together onstage with the cast, Ortel sat at a bank of

computers and watched the various monitors dance with abstract shapes. He looked like the navigator on the Starship Enterprise keeping his eye on the expansion, rotation, and revolution of a handful of distant galaxies. And his job is unique. A former lighting designer, he doesn't know of anyone else who does quite what he does, and he's been doing it for seven years.

Working on *The Little Mermaid* put him in close and continual contact with Natasha Katz, whose bank of computers was set up in the center of the house a little closer to the stage than his. "I'm always very reliant on the lighting designer," Ortel says, "for looking at scenes and seeing what works best and how we can create certain feelings or moods, and how we can give focus or take away focus. What I do is very similar to what lighting designers do. It's only that my material behaves differently and reacts differently to surfaces, and it comes only from one direction, which is from the front."

For Ortel, there are no limits on what he can do in his role. "I can become very cinematic if I want to," he says, "but what I do has to fit the language of the entire production. So if the set is very abstract, as this one is, the animation can't be highly naturalistic." In fact, the animated "stencils" that Ortel created were more stylistically appropriate than the real underwater footage he has taken as a diver. "When we first started out, I projected some of that film footage, and everybody

looked at it, but no one said anything. Then I showed them some of the cutout shapes I made, and it was, 'Oh, yeah, yeah, yeah, that's it!'" Sometimes the imitation of life seems more real than life itself.

"We're also trying to be fairly subtle in this production," says Ortel. "The audience isn't meant to be distracted by the projections, or even aware of them consciously. They work subliminally."

Subliminal or not, even digitally produced and abstract, the images are specific. "I took my cue from the shapes of the costumes and a lot of the shapes on George's sets. There are a lot of crescents, a lot of twisted pieces that wind up looking like crescents. So the shapes that I make and the ones that already exist mesh as well as they can. There are no photographs of bubbles, for example, but shapes that are generated to suggest or approximate bubbles and the way bubbles might make you feel. Actually, there aren't a lot of bubbles underwater, unless there's a diver nearby."

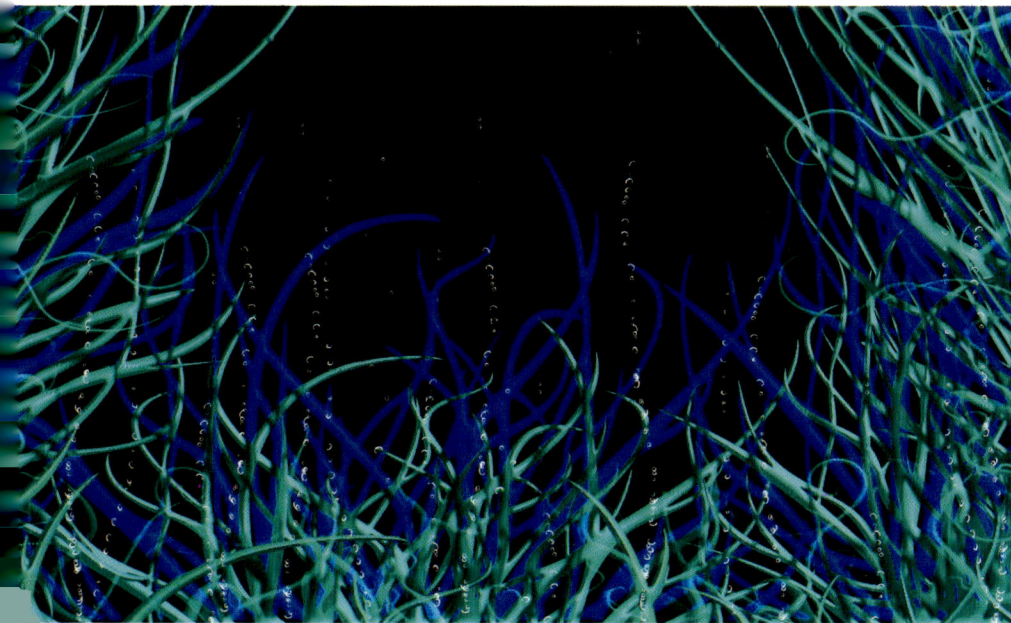

COSTUMES FOR THE LITTLE MERMAID were designed by Tatiana Noginova, who is from St. Petersburg, Russia. "Tom [Schumacher] and I were looking for a costume designer with a quirky voice," says Francesca Zambello, "but also a beautiful classical aesthetic, and who knew how to make costumes work. So I introduced him to Tanya. I had worked with her in Russia. She's not the first person you'd think of to design costumes for a musical, but she ran the costume shop at the Kirov Opera, so she's built thousands of costumes over fifteen years and designed them, too.

"That was in the summer of 2006. Tanya was in New York working on an opera at the Met. Tom liked her aesthetic and that she had so much hands-on experience. One of Tom's

great strengths is that his background as a craftsman comes into play so often, and that's a funny yin-yang thing that we have, where I'm, like, 'It's got to be like this, but I don't have the patience to think it through, and Tom just loves to get in there with the nuts and bolts. It's a good balance.

"So Tanya came on board and she started her process," relates Zambello. "She made a set of prototypes for a week-long workshop we decided to have in London, and she came from Russia with suitcases full of prototypes for the eels, for the Mersisters, for Ursula, and she had built them all herself in Moscow and brought them on the plane.

"We asked a lovely costume designer both Tom and I have worked with in London named Jackie Galloway to help out, and he got together a bunch of dancers that choreographer Stephen Mear and I both know, and we staged 'Under the Sea,' 'Kiss the Girl,' and 'She's in Love.' A lot of that was about working out the fantastical aspects of the costumes. But one big central thing that has always been important was making sure that Ariel is always the central character and that the actress always has prominence."

Zambello knew she had to coordinate the costume design and the show's choreographer early. The two contributed heavily to her overriding directorial concept. "To me, it's really key in all of these shows that take place in worlds different from our own, that the actor is paramount," says Zambello, "that we don't lose the actor. We don't cover the actor's face. We don't hide their own physicality. That's why a lot of the costumes have, you know, exposed chests and arms so that the actors are part human and part fantasy.

"The tricky thing about this show for costumes, which I don't think people ever think about, or realize, is that in other Disney shows, you're always in one world. In *Beauty and the Beast* everyone is an inanimate object that is animated. In *The Lion King*, every character is an animal. The tricky thing about *The Little Mermaid* is that we have three worlds. We have real people who are real people. We have actors playing animals the whole time. And we have merpeople, who are purely imaginary. So we have fantastical creatures, animals and humans, and we're trying to make a unified language for them. That's really always been the challenge of the piece, I think."

It was certainly a challenge to Stephen Mear, an award-winning West End and Broadway choreographer, whose credits include Disney's coproduction of *Mary Poppins* with the U.K.'s Cameron Mackintosh, for which he was nominated for a Tony. The recipient of multiple Olivier Awards for his work in London, Mear has created the dances for numerous classic as well as new musicals. And he'd worked with Zambello, on a production of Mozart's *Don Giovanni*

at Covent Garden and on a big pop concert at Cardiff's Millennium Stadium in Wales. Versatile enough to choreograph ballet and razzle-dazzle tap, Mear had the breadth and the experience to make dances for Alan Menken's artistic score.

He is also the man who came up with the idea of putting the *Mermaid* actors on wheels. "I was at Disneyland," remembers Mear, "when a little boy whizzed by. I literally chased after him to ask his parents what he was wearing on his feet. His parents thought I was mad." What the boy was wearing were Heelys, those athletic shoes with wheels in the heels that became a great rage among the preteen set.

"I said, 'Oh, my God, that's fantastic!'" Mear remembers, "and then I rang Francesca and said, 'We have to use them. They give us a language,' and the nice thing is that nobody's ever questioned it." Mear and the costumers came up with a version of the Heely, based on a high-heeled dance shoe, that the cast and crew nicknamed "merblades." (They were made by the entertainment industry's legendary cobbler Oscar Novarro in California.)

Mear was enthusiastic. "With these shoes you can pirouette, you can jeté, you can dance. You can't dance on roller skates. You can't be walking normally and then suddenly push off and glide like you've swum off somewhere. With these very special Heelys you can."

OPPOSITE: A preliminary costume/concept sketch for Ursula (more diva than cephalopod).
RIGHT: An early concept drawing by Tatiana Noginova.

"What you think looks good in your mind might not look good on your leading lady or leading man, and you have to change, because the movement has to come from their bodies, not the mind of the choreographer." —STEPHEN MEAR

"If someone says to me, 'There are three dance numbers in the show,' my immediate instinct is, 'I'm not the right choreographer for your show.' But Francesca sat me down," Mear recalls, "and said, 'You know, you'll have to choreograph scene changes and all that so there's a fluidity all the way through the show.' That's my kind of show. Even in the acting scenes we did our little bit—you know, working on Ariel's arms, for example, so it looked like she was underwater. We had to choreograph the tables for 'Les Poissons.' We even had to choreograph the lights in the wings. I've never seen so many lights in the wings."

In fact, the merblades, as they're sometimes dubbed by the cast, become part of the vocabulary of the show within moments after they first appear onstage, but they're a bit tricky to master. "Sierra Boggess was an ice-skater," Mear remembers, "so she didn't have too much trouble, and the kids playing Flounder were great because they have no fear, but they took some getting used to for the rest of the cast."

"You'd be standing there on wheels," reports Tyler Maynard, who created the role of Flotsam opposite Derrick Baskin's Jetsam, "and you'd hear a little cry behind you, and you knew someone was going down. Then you'd hear the crash as they hit the floor. The first costume they put Flotsam and Jetsam in had the hands sewn down to the body of the suit, and I said, 'I can't wear that, because I'm going to be falling down a lot, and I need my hands to get back up.'"

Part of the challenge for Mear was just how much choreography the show demanded. Not just the dance numbers, but nearly every aspect of what happens onstage or off was choreographed by Mear and associate choreographer Tara Young, who has worked on a dozen Broadway shows. But that, Mear says, is how he likes it.

But of course, the bulk of what the audience sees as choreography are the bigger production numbers like "Under the Sea" and "Kiss the Girl" (which involved choreographing the dancers around the moving set pieces, which have a choreography of their own). For those numbers there were antecedents in the 1989 film. But the stage version has many new numbers, and Mear had to start them from scratch. Scuttle's "Human Stuff" and "Positoovity" are among the new dance numbers, the latter of which is a comic tap number that appeals to Mear's dancing heart (note the highly successful "Step in Time" number he created for *Mary Poppins*).

Some of the show's dance numbers went through more evolution than others. "Under the Sea" was completely redone in the Denver out-of-town run in the summer of 2007. "Part of the challenge of that number is that so much is going on," says Mear, "but you have to keep the focus on Ariel. Choreography is just one of the ways you tell your story, and you have to be careful that you don't lose the story because the choreography is taking too much attention." But if "Under the Sea" was elusive, "She's in Love" was not. "When I heard 'She's in Love,' I knew what I was going to do straight away," Mear says. "There was no homework, no research, no fretting. I just did it. Francesca started by staging the first little

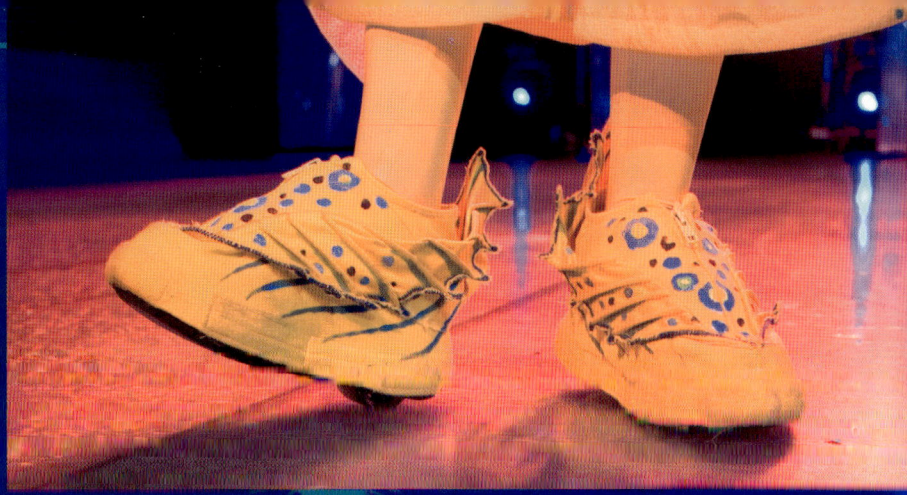

Eels on Wheels

THE ROLLING SHOES THAT some of *The Little Mermaid* characters wear on stage are custom adaptations of Heelys, the wildly popular sneaker with the wheel in the heel first patented by Roger Adams in 2000. In *The Little Mermaid*, only the boys who play Flounder wear actual Heelys, but you can't buy them in a store: the shoes are dressed up in what assistant costume designer Brian J. Bustos calls "spats," a kind of slipcover for footwear that matches the actors' costumes.

The adult members of the cast wear special custom adaptations of Heelys that are made by master cobbler Oscar Navarro. He is the legendary owner of Capri Shoes in Fullerton, California, and specializes in novelty shoes for film and television. He makes all the character shoes for the Disney theme parks and also made the seagull's tap-dancing "clown" shoes for *The Little Mermaid*.

Navarro worked from costume designer Tatiana Noginova's description and technical drawings to create the first of several prototypes for the finished shoes, which take a minimum of four weeks per pair to make—by hand. The housing mechanism and the wheels come from Heelys, but they are specially engineered for *The Little Mermaid* with greater backward mobility to accommodate the choreography. And they employ the widest wheel made by Heelys so they won't sink into the scenery tracks. Heelys makes silver-toned wheels with no branding on them for the show. The wheels are changed often so they always look fresh and function perfectly. "They ship them to us by the carton," says Bustos—and they even get a credit in the *Playbill*: Gliding by Heelys®.

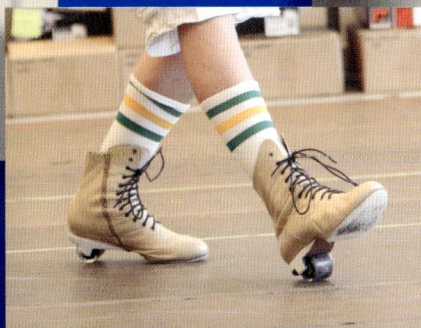

TOP: Flounder's Heelys ("spats" over commercially available shoes). ABOVE: Shoes for the adults were custom designed and made by legendary cobbler Oscar Navarro. RIGHT: Choreographer Stephen Mear goes for a spin.

Choreographer Stephen Mear, master of many styles, teaches *The Little Mermaid* cast its dance moves, including Sherie Rene Scott (TOP CENTER), Eddie Korbich (TOP RIGHT), and Tyler Maynard (BOTTOM CENTER).

scene, and then I took over. The final number as it plays in the show is nearly the same as it was in that first workshop we did in London.

"Sometimes you plan a whole dance out in advance, and then you have to change everything because what you had in your mind doesn't work for the dancers you have when the rehearsals start. What you think looks good in your mind might not look good on your leading lady or leading man, and you have to change, because the movement has to come from their bodies, not the mind of the choreographer."

"Positoovity," for example, became a featured tap number not just because Stephen Mear loves tap but also because Eddie Korbich, the show's first Scuttle, is an adept tap dancer. In fact, much of Mear's choreography adopts the strengths

of his actors. "One Step Closer" has as much dancing in it because Sierra Boggess and Sean Palmer both have dance training. "It's a real luxury when the young lovers can actually dance," says Mear. More often they are cast for their acting and singing abilities, with dance talent thrown in as an afterthought.

In fact, the very idea of a "One Step Closer" number was Mear's. "I said, 'Shouldn't we do a little dance here that's about learning to communicate without words?' And Alan came back with this beautiful 'One Step Closer' number where the two of them are falling in love and it's not about her voice. It's about two hearts speaking to each other without words." In fact, Mear is ideally suited to conceive of such a storytelling strategy: his life partner is deaf. (Mear also came up with the idea of using sign language for the "Supercalifragilisticexpialidocious" number in *Mary Poppins*).

"You know, I always think that choreography is successful when people in the audience sit there and think, 'I could do that' or at least, 'I'd like to have a go at that.' As a choreographer I'm not trying to say, 'Look at me.' I'm trying to say, 'Look at the story.' The choreography is a means to that end, not the end itself."

Another fact of life in the creation of a Broadway musical is that time restraints mean people are working simultaneously on things that have a great impact on other things. "You can see a drawing of a dance costume," says producer Thomas Schumacher, "and it's diaphanous, and when the costume shows up, it's practically upholstered. It's nobody's fault. It's just two sets of expectations not gelling. Something has to change, either the choreography or the costume."

But if the costume changes, the lighting may also need to change. Sometimes a line of dialogue has to change. Change in the lighting might mean changing the projection. A Broadway musical is a carefully balanced ecology midwifed by humans. It's also like a giant sudoku puzzle: if you change one square, the whole grid has to be reconstructed.

Some of the costumes built for *The Little Mermaid* were too heavy or bulky or stiff for the movement. Fish tails had to be rigged so that other actors didn't wheel into them dragging on the ground. The seagulls' tap shoes were made bigger and bigger to up the ante on the comedy until they were virtually clown shoes. But these were so hard to tap in that you couldn't hear the taps from out in the house. The seagull ensemble was finally given the smaller version of the tap boots they had started out in (except for Scuttle, who had mastered the art of big-shoe tap).

BELOW LEFT: John Treacy Egan. BELOW CENTER: Tara Young and Stephen Mear. BOTTOM RIGHT: Tim Federle. BOTTOM CENTER: Sierra Boggess and Sean Palmer.

One Step Closer

"I said, 'Shouldn't we do a little dance here that's about learning to communicate without words?'" —STEPHEN MEAR

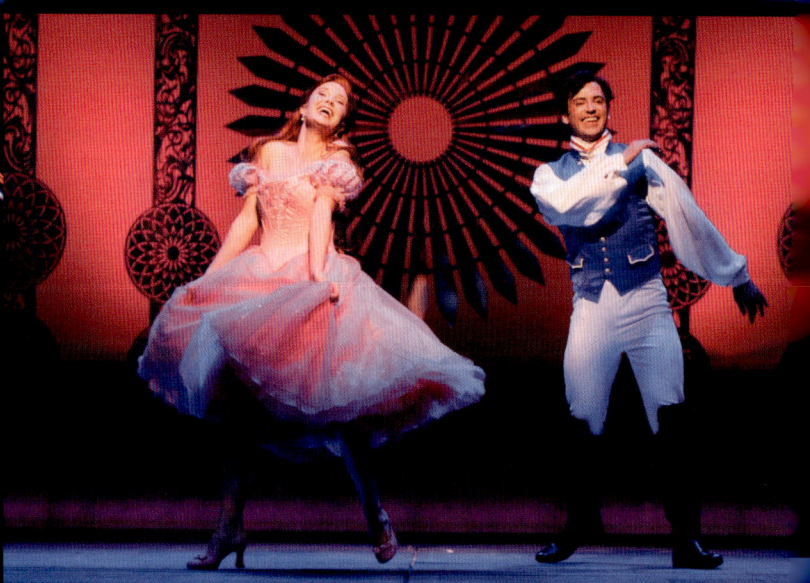

OPPOSITE: Costume sketch for Ariel
by Tatiana Noginova.

THERE ARE MANY KINDS of costumes, but they fall into a few general types: historical, contemporary, and fantasy. Clearly, the costumes for *The Little Mermaid* fall into the last category (with a good dose of crossover). They are extremely important for many reasons. For one thing, they identify the characters. They enhance the storytelling. They help establish the mood of any given scene. They can be funny or beautiful or both at the same time. Sometimes they need to visually carry a scene or (in the case of *The Little Mermaid*) to distinguish land creatures from sea creatures—and they must blend into the overall look of the production.

The evolution of the costume design for *The Little Mermaid* took nearly three years. Designer Tatiana Noginova, another of Francesca Zambello's opera connections (who had also worked with George Tsypin), created three entire sets of drawings, hundreds of built pieces, some of which were rebuilt more than once and some of which were simply dropped from the show (like the costumes for the mermen that existed in the script until the out-of-town run in Denver and were dropped thereafter).

An aspiring dancer as a child, Noginova turned to design after she broke her leg at age twelve. As an adult, she's worked in costume shops for banner companies in Russia, including the Mariinsky Theatre in St. Petersburg and the Bolshoi in Moscow, but *The Little Mermaid* is her first musical. And although it is not her biggest production—that honor goes to the 1,200 costumes of Prokofiev's *War and Peace*—she estimates its difficulty and the amount of work involved, as very much equivalent to that epic Russian opera.

Working at first "in the dark" after seeing Tsypin's models for the set, Noginova had little idea of the limits or parameters of her assignment. But she did have some close-at-hand inspiration. "In Russia," she says, "we have a lot of fairy tales about mermaids. Russians love these creatures." In conceptualizing the look of her mermaids for the show, Noginova was delighted to find in her research that there are basically two kinds of mermaids: "Saltwater and freshwater," she jokes, explaining that the ocean mermaids have fish tails and can only swim, but the river variety have legs and can walk on land as well as live under the water.

Happily, the realm of fantasy gives a designer room to invent whatever she or he likes—so long as it is convincing to an audience. And mermaids with legs and Heelys as well as tails simply didn't seem too incongruous to the creative team—and audiences seem to have no trouble accepting the creatures at all. After all, this is a work of the imagination, not of marine biology. In a fantasy, your imagination is the only limit. And it is in that spirit that Noginova made her first set of sketches.

To get her creative juices flowing, Noginova did something quite real. She went diving in the Red Sea. "And the first thing I noticed was that the color you lose under the water is red. It's all blue and green and a bit of yellow—less color than we have onstage now."

"We have fantastical creatures, animals, and humans, and we're trying to make a unified language for them. That's really always been the challenge of the piece. . . ."
—TATIANA NOGINOVA

Some of the changes made in the costumes were for practical considerations. For one thing, the early costume conceit was that these merpeople could change their clothing, so that there could be a formal look or a more casual look. Then the costumes were sent out to bid, and the bottom line was considerably over budget. Noginova and her crew started looking for ways to economize without damaging the concept. Changing clothes was deemed unimportant to the main story of Ariel. The idea was scratched and has never been missed.

Like everything else in a Broadway show, the costumes are a collaboration. The Ursula costume, for example, which took a year to build "because everyone was one hundred percent in the process," says Noginova, including the actress playing her (Sherie Rene Scott). "Sherie was also part of the design team," Noginova says, "because she understood completely what she needed to do in the costume and what you could get rid of and what you had to keep if you didn't want to kill the costume. It was great to have this kind of a relationship with an actress."

Sometimes costumes change because new information comes to the designer. "Suddenly you find out that the actor

Costume associate Tracy Christensen (whose extensive Broadway experience made up for Noginova's neophyte status) came onto the project after the second set of costume sketches, amendments to the first set after discussions with Zambello, Tsypin, Mear, and Schumacher. "Some of those costumes didn't change very much from the sketches," says Christensen, "but some changed quite a bit."

One of the major changes was to the costume of Ursula. "The first Ursula sketch I saw," says Christensen, "was very operatic, in presentation and scale, and I think part of the challenge of switching over to a musical-theater setting is that people are talking and singing, and you have to be able to relate to them differently than you relate to an operatic character." You also have to build them differently. Opera costumes may be worn once or twice a season. Theater costumes are worn eight times a week, fifty-two weeks a year. They have to be much more durable.

has to do something onstage he cannot do in the costume you have designed." Sometimes small changes are made each day until the designer looks at what is left and realizes that all the life has been taken out of it and she has to go back to the drawing board and reconceive it.

"Well, it's kind of where we got with Flotsam and Jetsam," says Christensen. "I mean we cut the heck out of it, and finally we had to just say, 'Okay, we're kind of at the end of the line here with this garment. We can start over, but we're pretty much at the capacity this garment has to withstand change.'"

A lot of work went into the show, of course, that no one in the audience will ever know. Like the number of reds Noginova went through before she came up with the red of Sebastian's costume. Or the fabric treatments she and her subcontractors were able to come up with to increase the underwater iridescence of a variety of fabrics. She didn't exactly invent new fabrics, she says, but she certainly looked far and wide for the most avant-garde textile treatments she could find in the industry.

Costume construction is expensive, and you can't usually fix a costume for five dollars and a roll of thread. "We had a terrible situation with our jellyfish costumes for 'Under the Sea,'" Christensen remembers. "They had been made in a really amazing beadwork manner, but it just wasn't working. It was too heavy. It wasn't moving right, and then they started falling apart and shooting beads all over the stage, and the

tech guys were freaking out because the beads were getting in the tracks in the deck so the scenery couldn't move. So there we were in the middle of Denver, and luckily the woman who made the costumes was there, too, so she grabbed Tanya [Noginova] and went off to the mall. They came back with a big bag of stuff from a sewing shop. They made new jellyfish skirts in a day, and those are the ones that are in the show now."

Scuttle's costume changed, too. "It was really, really hot," says actor Eddie Korbich. "It had a coat that I would never put on until just before I went onstage because it was so heavy. And I had no wings. I really wanted wings so I could flap them, even though I knew I wasn't going to fly." Scuttle got his wings: in fact, all the seagulls got new costumes between Denver and Broadway.

The sheer number of things tried and rejected is almost unfathomable, as is the microscopic scale at which the entire creative staff considers each detail. At one point all the seagulls were wearing their beak hats at a jaunty hip-hop angle. Producer Thomas Schumacher straightened them all out, leaving only Scuttle with a skewed visor. And that wasn't the only change of headgear. At one point in the development of the show Sebastian had a very tiny hat that held his microphone (the actor has a shaved pate so the mike couldn't be hidden in a wig), but it seemed impossible to keep the hat glued on the actor's head.

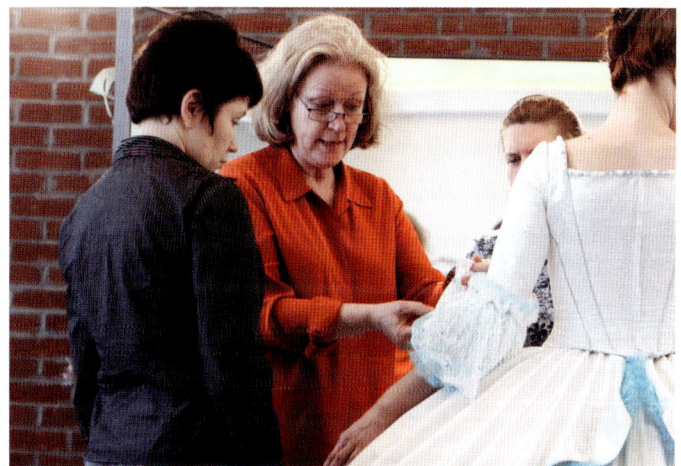

TOP: Associate costumer designer Tracy Christensen.
ABOVE: Tatiana Noginova consults with Katherine Marshall of Tricorne on an early fitting

An Undersea Gallery

Designs by Tatiana Noginova

костюм
пузырей

OPPOSITE: Sherie Rene Scott

OPPOSITE: Norm Lewis

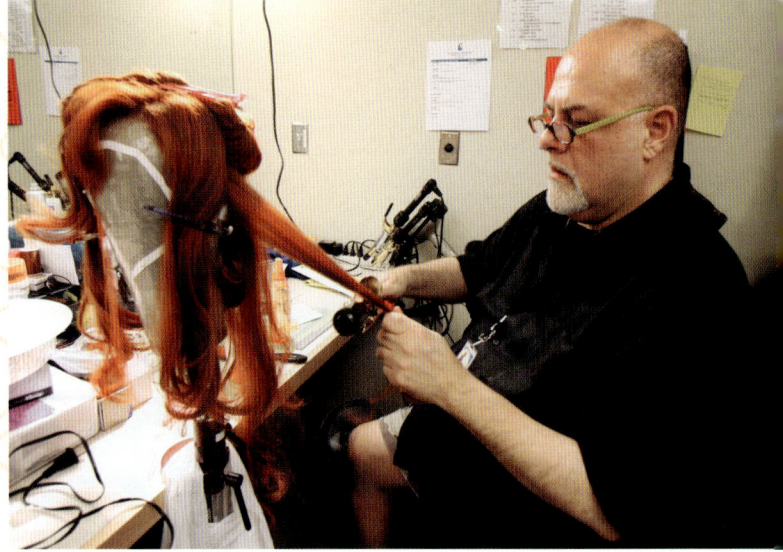

LEFT: Hair supervisor Thomas Augustine fits Sierra Boggess for one of Ariel's three wigs.
ABOVE: Tom dresses the wig between shows.

THE TASK OF KEEPING SEBASTIAN'S hat glued to his shaven pate, for a reason known only to the angels who divvy up the work assignments on musicals, fell to hair designer David Brian Brown, a veteran of many Broadway shows, including several of Disney's. Working closely with makeup designer Angelina Avallone, he was responsible for many of the final touches on the actors. More than visual clues for the audience, how an actor feels in his or her wig and makeup helps define the roles for the performers.

Part of Brown's assignment was to contribute to the feeling of an underwater flow. "At first we actually thought about wigs that would look like they were floating under the water," Brown says, but that just proved to be impossible. We settled on a wig for Ariel that would have a lot of movement in it. And, of course, there was the question of what color red to make her hair," which meant Brown had to interface with lighting designer Natasha Katz.

"Obviously," Brown summarizes, "colored lights affect the colors of the objects they light. And blue lighting on stage, which you would think of as normal for an underwater reality, turns anything red to brown. So we were concerned that our famously red-haired mermaid look like she has red hair. "We

did an early prototype on Ariel, and it was a disaster, for me. We did it a true red, really cool, so it was a blue-red. Tom and Francesca absolutely hated it. So then we went with a much more ginger red, and we then ran bright red highlights through it to kind of pop it and give it the color that it is now.

As it happens, Ariel wears several different wigs during the show so that a single wig doesn't need to be restyled several times in the course of one performance, which also enables the actress to make faster changes. But there is only one makeup design for this leading lady, because she is onstage so much of the time.

"She doesn't have time to change it," says Avallone. "Once Ariel is in that makeup, she stays in that makeup until the end of the show. So the makeup has to work with the different wigs, different costumes, different scenes, different lighting. She can't just duck out for a touch-up. She barely has time to change her costumes."

Avallone coordinated an entire light test for the hair and makeup departments—a mock-up that included the materials used on the set—so that she could see something like the final lighting when she was designing the makeup looks. She also trained the actors in how to do their own makeup, except for Ursula, who has help.

"It takes about an hour to get Ursula ready, between makeup and hair," says Avallone, "and we have to coordinate the hair and the makeup because while we're doing certain parts of the makeup, the wig can go on, but we have to start first with certain parts of the face, forehead, foundation. And then there is a point where we can switch around, where the hairstylist can work to the front or to the side of the wig and then we can paint her neck, because we paint the back of the neck and part of her back with makeup.

ABOVE: Sketches for makeup designs by Angelina Avallone.
BELOW: Some of the many false eyelashes used for the show.

Like costumes, wigs can change in the course of a show's development. The exaggerated wigs the young ladies in the second-act singing contest wear were designed by Noginova and made by Brown. They're elaborate, and comedic, but they have remained pretty much the same from conception to opening night. Meanwhile Triton's hair changed a lot.

"Originally we did it all white, as it is in the film," says Brown. "Our idea was to make him look more natural, but it didn't make him look natural. It made him look more like a cartoon. Tom and Francesca thought he should be younger,

less like Ariel's grandfather. So, I went out and I bought a lot of hair in a lot of different textures, and we gave him dreadlocks and some bluish green curls. And then we totally eliminated his full beard."

"His makeup changed, too," says Avallone. We added some blue highlights, and gold and copper, and we did some body makeup to show off his body since they took away the top of his costume at one point and left his torso bare."

"In terms of makeup, the ensemble members have their work cut out for them," Avallone continues, "because they have a lot of changes. They change their costumes up to nine times. Sometimes they go back to a costume they wore before. I discovered early in the process that the only way we could transform them was by layering. They don't have time to take makeup off during act one or act two, but they can put something new on, change their lipstick, for example.

"We put glitter on the lipstick. We use a lot of eyelashes. We probably researched every eyelash available on the market. The swans in 'Kiss the Girl' have special lashes from France. They're very long, with iridescent white feathers. During the intermission they take everything off and start over again."

Makeup designer Angelina Avallone tested various designs as part of the process of creating Ursula's final appearance.

Sherie Rene Scott takes a moment to consider Avallone's cosmetic artistry.

Hair designer David Brian Brown puts the finishing touches on Ursula's wig.

Sherie Rene Scott

Tentacle Rehearsal

IF IT'S NOT EASY BEING green, as a certain famous Muppet frog once sang, imagine how difficult it is to be green and to have six or eight larger-than-life tentacles coming out of your body. Film Ursula could change size and shape; theater Ursula must rely on costume, set, and lighting wizardry to fill the stage with her sea-witchery. To give the devilish denizen of the deep her due, she not only wears tentacles (on two different costumes), but they also grow from her spherical pod of a home. Additionally, supersized serpentine tentacles sprout from the proscenium arch to reach out and embrace the audience with their up-to-no-good undulations.

The first of Ursula's two multi-limbed costumes has six arms—or are they legs?—and is called the "floating" costume by the costume staff because the six constructed tentacles float off the floor (the actress's arms represent the seventh and eighth). Each of the tentacles is precisely calibrated and engineered (by Jon Gellman) to be movable both up and down and back and forth, each to a different degree so they don't get tangled up in each other. The second costume, the "flip-up" has eight legs and folds like a fan (or a peacock tail) behind the show's tuneful villainess when it's not unfurled to resemble a giant spiderweb.

Both the set and the costume tentacles are based on Chinese folding paper puzzles and those honeycomb-like foldout Halloween pumpkins or wedding bells that are used as party decorations. The folding and unfolding of Ursula's appendages are part of a general concept developed by set designer George Tsypin to recall the movements of flexible plants and animals that live in the ocean and move with the sea's currents. They are also specially painted to glow an eerie green under the black lights, which are part of Natasha Katz's lighting design.

OPPOSITE: Sherie Rene Scott and Tyler Maynard.
LEFT: Sherie Rene Scott in Ursula's "flip-up" costume. ABOVE: The "floating" costume, with tentacles that dangle off the floor.

LEFT, ABOVE, AND RIGHT:
Sherie Rene Scott rehearses "I Want the Good Times Back" along with Stephen Mear, Derrick Baskin, and Tyler Maynard.

ONE OF THE HARDEST THINGS to convey about the production of a Broadway-scale stage musical is the enormous amount of work that goes into it, most of which is never seen—and that doesn't include the years of development (seven for *The Little Mermaid*).

Rehearsals were held six days a week, but there was rarely only one rehearsal in progress at a time. The director could be staging one number with the choreographer and ensemble while the music director worked on songs with the principals in another studio with associate choreographer Tara Young and associate music director Greg Anthony, and associate director Brian Hill staged a new acting scene elsewhere. The "associates" in a Broadway show are much like the vice president in the government, except they work as much and as often as the president.

"Tara and Brian were my right and left hands as we put *Mermaid* together," says Francesca Zambello. "Tara is able to speak in the language of movement and choreography so that anyone can learn it. Brian, who has a canny sense of words, was invaluable in the script development. He's also a fine actor himself, so I would often have him read all the roles when we were working out a scene."

Associate producer Todd Lacy was charged with keeping every detail of each department of the show working seam-

lessly with the others (not an easy task). The associate designers—Peter Eastman for sets, Tracy Christensen for costumes, Yael Lubetzky for lighting—not only participate in making design decisions but are often the individuals who oversee the nuts-and-bolts translation of a design from concept to stage. Naturally, all of this simultaneous work needs a great deal of coordination. Enter production supervisor Clifford Schwartz—a Disney veteran and one of Broadway's most beloved professionals—with his stage management crew headed by stage manager Theresa Bailey.

"These people all work incredibly hard and are enormously talented," says Thomas Schumacher (their colleague and their boss). "The show simply would not have been possible without their enormous contributions."

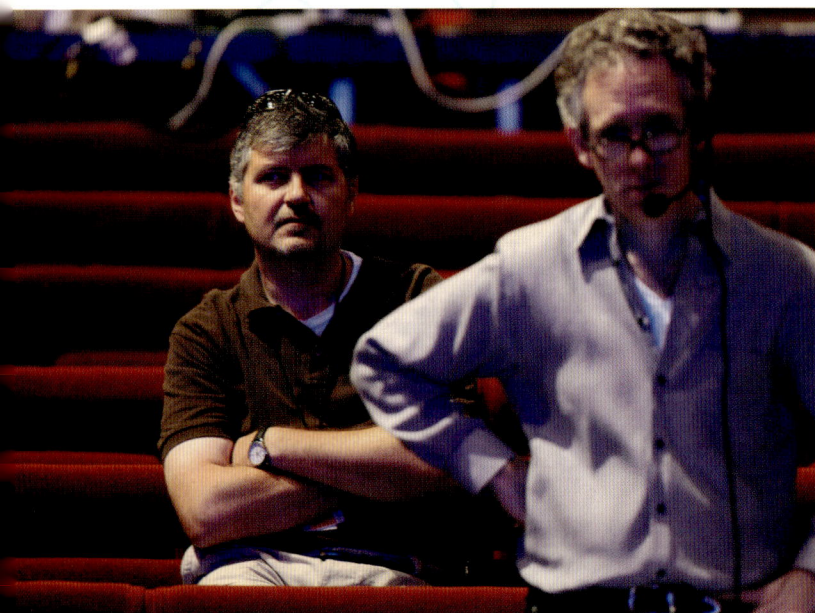

TOP: Production supervisor Clifford Schwartz and associate director Brian Hill discuss the rehearsal schedule. LEFT: Associate producer Todd Lacy, along with Clifford Schwartz, takes in a rehearsal.

Meanwhile, the costumes were being designed and built, as were the sets. The costumes were not all built in one place, so the designers were constantly on the move from one shop to another and having skirts and vests and petticoats sent by messenger or shipped from afar. The set pieces were made not only all over the city, but all over the continent, from Canada to the workshops of the Disney Imagineers in California, which meant a lot of coordination for the design staff. Props were made or ordered by Jerry L. Marshall, dozens of microphones were tested and loaded with batteries (sound designer John Shivers and crew), and all the sound equipment for the theater ordered and installed (all the stage work under the supervision of technical director, David Benken).

Needless to say, music doesn't arrive in the orchestra pit on opening night as a first draft. For one thing, there's a rehearsal band to hire. The pit orchestra needs to be assembled, too. Typically, the composer and lyricist write and rewrite songs as the book writer makes revisions. For this production, Michael Kosarin is credited as "Music Director, Incidental Music & Vocal Arrangements." But he is far from alone in the music department, which has been coordinated by Michael Keller. Koz was backed up at rehearsals by Greg Anthony, conducting the rehearsal combo and accommodating changes made on the spot or between rehearsals.

Mermaid had a dance arranger, too (David Chase) and the renowned Danny Troob on orchestrations. Most of the music work is done on computer and moved around the city, and the world, by e-mail. Rodgers and Hammerstein would need some crash courses on the iMac to work in theater today (possibly from *Mermaid*'s synth programmer, Andy Barrett).

There's a company manager, too, Disney Theatrical Production's Randy Meyer, and various individuals credited with magic and illusion, fly automation, and aerial design (the Argentine director Pichon Baldinú, who also created the flying for *Tarzan*). Where there are children, of course, there is a

Associate choreographer Tara Young

chaperone as well as an accredited tutor and, for this production, a children's vocal coach as well as a dialogue and vocal coach for the adult actors (Deborah Hecht). There are advertising and publicity and merchandising people around, too, in addition to the executive staff, attorneys, and accountants—and a good deal of all this activity is photographed and videotaped not just for the Disney archives but for television and print ads—and this book.

And almost all of everything each of these people does gets done over and over again—sometimes after hours of spirited discussion—until it all begins to come together.

And then, sometimes, the production moves out of town.

THE LITTLE MERMAID LEFT THE region of Broadway and 42nd Street at the beginning of July 2007 (Sunday the first was the official "travel day"). The company headed west, to the 2,225-seat Ellie Caulkins Opera House at the Denver Center for the Performing Arts (it's a 2005 renovation of the century-old Auditorium Theater, which was the site of the 1908 Democratic National Convention). They would rehearse for five weeks before moving into the theater for tech rehearsals for another three and half. There would be twenty-six previews (from July 26 to August 22) and twenty-one regular performances (August 23 to September 9).

Shows go out of town for a lot of reasons. Generally it is to finish a production that is within sight of its goals but not yet finished. Part of the finishing process involves performing the show in front of an audience to gauge its reactions: if the audience doesn't laugh, the joke's not working.

"When we did the show in Denver," reports Doug Wright, "we invited a group of eight- to twelve-year-olds to see it. Then we asked them to assess it afterward, and they were so trenchant. They were like, well, 'King Triton's like my

dad. He's torn between work and giving sufficient time and attention to his family.' And everything seemed to resonate for them. It's so easy in children's stories to condescend, but children balk at that. They resist it."

An out-of-town run can also help boost the confidence of the cast. There's nothing like a nightly standing ovation in a sold-out house—which was *Mermaid*'s experience in Denver—to make everyone feel good about all the hard work. It can also be confusing and disorienting. Not only does the show have to go through the difficult cue-by-cue technical rehearsal period for a theater it will play in only briefly, but the cast and crew are in temporary housing in an unfamiliar city. They rehearse during the day and perform at night: sometimes the changes they rehearse in the afternoon go into the show that night, sometimes not. (Sherie Rene Scott reports that Ursula's changes were coming so fast and furiously that to keep up with them she was writing new lines on her hands.)

A pre-Broadway tryout is a great place to see what works and what doesn't, and it's usually considered a treat for local audiences to see a show in its earliest stages. But it's a lot of hard work. Oddly, the cast and crew of Mermaid are quite low-key in their description of the Denver process, although they might have been a bit more stressed at the time.

Shortly after the Broadway opening of *The Little Mermaid*, director Francesca Zambello hosted a party at her Upper West Side apartment in New York City for the cast. She was shocked to hear them remembering Denver as a lot of fun. "And I was just asking myself," Zambello relates, "is this the same cast that was complaining, 'Why do we have to be here?' in Denver. So a lot gets filtered out of the memory. And an out-of-town run is a great bonding experience for a cast, because they're all thrown into something new and uncomfortable together."

Most shows change a great deal out of town. A few change relatively little. How much *The Little Mermaid* changed depends on whom you ask.

"One of the things we focused on in Denver," says Wright, was, as exuberant as the show was, it didn't have an innate build, so the audience didn't get carried along on that wave of excitement we knew was buried in the show. We needed to rebuild the show in such a way that it had a cumulative growth until if finally exploded. I think Stephen re-choreographed 'Under the Sea' to astonishing effect."

"Oh, we went through many different versions of 'Under the Sea,'" Stephen Mear agrees. "The first one, the one we rehearsed in New York and did at Denver was, I think, too busy too early. You know, whenever you bring on a large scenic piece like one of George's columns, it tends to pull your focus, so you have to make sure that you're telling the story with Ariel. And you can't pull the focus from her by bringing two big jellyfish on straightaway. In the film that song was done all in little vignettes. But onstage you have to tell this whole ministory inside the story. I actually went to Sea World because I was so obsessed about trying to get this number right. We were changing things all the time. We never stopped changing things."

In Denver the set was in a state of constant evolution and was never actually finished to the degree it was finished for the Broadway production. Costumes changed a lot. Even Ariel got new costumes.

"One day Tom came in and said, 'Ariel needs a big fabulous sparkly wedding dress,'" reports costume associate Tracy Christensen. "And Tanya said, 'I don't get it. Why?' It's not a thing in her world. And Tom said, 'You know what? It's a Disney-princess thing. It's an American musical-theater thing. Trust me.' So she tried to take the American convention and infuse it with some of her more Russian sensibility."

And it's not enough that the costumes look good and harmonize with all the other visuals and suit the actors, they also have to hold up during stunts, and those changed, especially as the ending of the show continued to evolve.

"Without giving away the surprise," says Christensen, "there's a costume that was added at the end of the show, and it has to magically disappear. We had to really pull some shenanigans with the construction of this thing, and when Ariel goes back to having a tail, the tail doesn't go on the same way all the other tails go on the other costumes, and it's smaller because it has to be hidden. Of course, a child Francesca knows came to the show and the first thing she said was, 'Why is that tail different?'"

Kids not only say the darndest things . . . they see everything. "Well, says Christensen, "it's like Andersen's 'The Emperor's New Clothes.' Adults see what they're told to see. Kids don't know what they're supposed to be seeing, so they just take it all in the way it really is."

OPPOSITE: Rehearsing "Human Stuff" in Denver.
RIGHT: Directors and choreographers in rehearsal (from left): Brian Hill, Francesca Zambello, Stephen Mear, Tara Young.

Producer Thomas Schumacher has his own perspective on the Denver tryout and why it didn't seem traumatic to the cast to be making as many changes as were actually accomplished. "Well, part of the reason is that we just didn't allow for backstage drama," he says. "We changed a lot. We cut, we moved, we redid, we added. Ursula's whole costume wasn't even there and working. Ursula's pod didn't have tentacles on it at all.

"We made many changes in Denver just getting physical things to work, getting the show to play. When we got it up on its feet we realized we needed to change quite a few things. But we kept the focus on the work, on telling the story. Doug was rewriting every day. He would send me new dialogue, and I would scribble on it things like, 'This isn't clear enough, what about something like this?' I mean, for a Pulitzer Prize–winning playwright, he was extremely open to being edited and to reworking things until he got them just the way he wanted them. We'd go back and forth until we both had what we needed from a scene.

"Denver didn't seem to be a terrible traumatic experience—which an out-of-town run can—because we just kept saying, 'This is what we're going to do,' and we just plugged away and we did it. We didn't have any fights about anything. If something wasn't working, we changed it. We cut sections of songs, we reconceived scenes. We combined scenes. We kept cutting and cutting to make it all leaner and more direct. And we did a lot of changes to the costumes. We would be literally tearing pieces off the costumes to let the actors loose. I would actually say we did more to *The Little Mermaid* than we've ever done to a show out of town.

"Another thing that made it seem painless was that the audience loved the show from day one. Sold out every night. Standing ovation every night. So there wasn't any hysteria about there not being a show in the material. We knew there was a show, and we knew we hadn't nailed the ending. Alan Menken in particular kept saying, 'I just don't care about the ending yet.'

"We hadn't captured the empowerment that Ariel had to achieve by the end of her journey. We hadn't captured the emotional density or complexity we were hoping for. So we kept reworking it. In one version Ursula flooded the ballroom, and Ariel stayed human—she didn't revert to being a mermaid at all. And we worried about how she would work herself out of her dilemma."

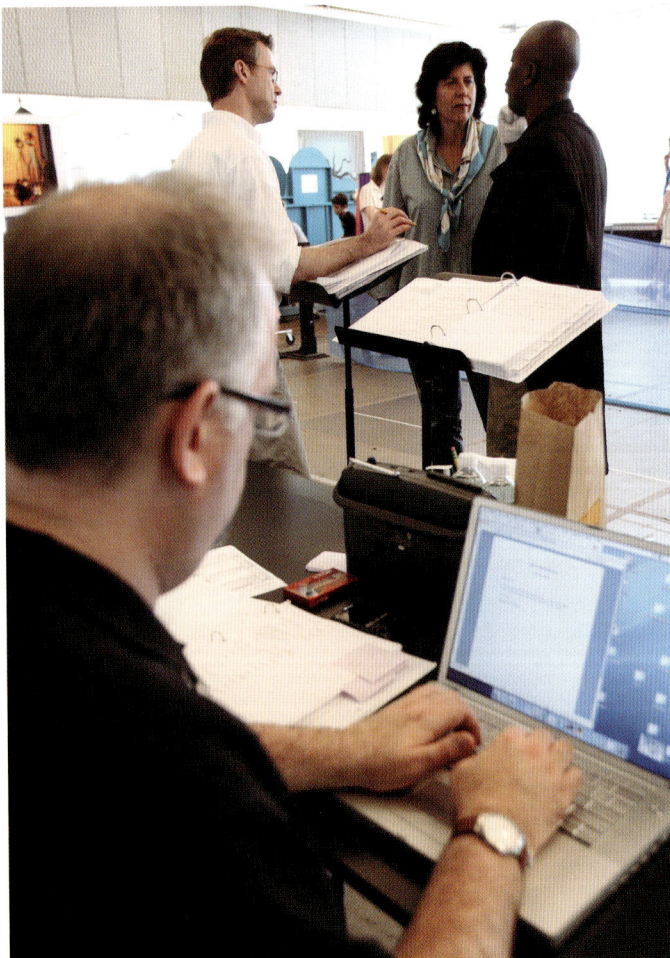

TOP: The producer and the director put their heads together.
LEFT: Doug Wright rewrites while Brian Hill and
Francesca Zambello rehearse with Tituss Burgess.
OPPOSITE: Sierra Boggess and Norm Lewis.

It was also clear from the Denver run that the show still needed work before the New York opening. "I think we all collectively agreed that the opening of the show needed to tighten by about five or seven minutes," says Doug Wright. "It was taking the first act a long time to levitate. And we wanted to make sure that we started with the requisite bang. So we retooled the first ten minutes of the show, getting to the musical number 'Human Stuff' a lot faster. And that was basically about compressing dialogue, compressing music, and also creating more dynamic visuals to bring us into the world.

"As for the ending, I came to see that there were certain plot moments in the film that I had ignored, but that proved to be indispensable. And one of those was that Triton, out of love for his daughter, restores her to human form, so she can in fact marry the prince. That beat was absent in Denver. And watching it again and again, and listening to Alan's concerns about the ending, it became evident that it's a really critical moment in the story, and the story doesn't feel emotionally true until that can happen."

Meanwhile, Schumacher and Zambello took the bull by the horns over Labor Day weekend of 2007. "We met in one of the big rooms at the theater in Denver and we tried to conceive of the ending we needed, just the two of us. We acted it out as a pantomime, beat by beat. We timed out how long things would take. We dealt with changing Ariel back into a mermaid, and where Ursula would go when she was vanquished, all of that," says Schumacher, who, it is worth noting, is a far more hands-on producer than most. "And one of the reasons why it all came together was that Alan and Glenn and Doug and Francesca and Stephen were all really willing to take things on."

The last show in Denver, on September 9, was followed by a three-week cast layoff. Suddenly, after more than three months hard labor and not more than one day off a week, the cast was able to relax, recuperate, and regroup. Rehearsals resumed in New York City on Monday, October 1; the cast moved into the Nederlander's 1,415-seat Lunt-Fontanne on October 15.

"We changed a lot. We cut, we moved, we redid, we added. . . . We made many changes in Denver just getting physical things to work, getting the show to play. When we got it up on its feet we realized we needed to change quite a few things. But we kept the focus on the work, on telling the story."

—THOMAS SCHUMACHER

THE FIRST PREVIEW, ON SATURDAY evening, November 3, went well. There was still work to do, particularly on the end of the show, but the creative team was focused. Opening night was scheduled for Thursday, December 6, 2007. That gave the creative team plenty of time to make even more changes.

"Ursula's role changed a lot," reports director Francesca Zambello. "Originally 'I Want the Good Times Back' was not her first song. The original song was much darker, but it didn't really help tell the story. What we always wanted to understand was the relationship between Ursula and Triton and why Ursula wanted Ariel so much. And so we finally came out with a real villainess's 'I want' song, which is antithetical to what you would normally think structurewise. At first we staged it very simply. The idea was it was a sad little production number with just her and her two eels. And then we added the other eels when we came to New York to make it more into a quote/unquote production number, like her fantasy."

"You get a lot of information from audience reactions," Zambello says, which is why previews are important. The director has noted distinct differences in the reaction to the show between adults and children. "Adults love Ursula. You can tell if there are a lot of adults in the audience with your eyes closed, because Ursula's jokes get much bigger laughs. When there are all-kid days, suddenly Flounder becomes much more important—almost as much of a protagonist as Ariel."

In fact, Zambello continues, one of the reasons things change in the course of a show's development is the actor cast in the role—which is why creating a role leaves a permanent mark on a character. Ursula changes a great deal between the film and the show for reasons that have to do with the changes in medium and the evolution of Ariel's story. Ursula also owes a lot to actress Sherie Rene Scott, one of the cast's most seasoned Broadway performers.

"Sherie brought a lot of herself to the work. We did a lot of improvisations around the characters in rehearsals, and she brought a lot to them that eventually went into the script. The humor evolved very much during the process as we saw what really worked and what didn't work. That's what was so great about having Doug as a collaborator. He's an on-site writer. He was there."

"As a director, it's important to use the actor. The actor is your clay. They're your conduit. Nothing should go onstage without going through the filter of their being. I love performances where I feel that the role and the performer have an amazing symbiotic relationship, that the performance only exists because it's that person in that role. The more they're giving of themselves, the more the audience responds. We're hungry for that kind of uniqueness. It's like a personal gift from

> "As a director, it's important to use the actor. The actor is your clay. They're your conduit. Nothing should go onstage without going through the filter of their being. I love performances where I feel that the role and the performer have an amazing symbiotic relationship, that the performance only exists because it's that person in that role"
>
> —FRANCESCA ZAMBELLO

ABOVE AND OPPOSITE: Sherie Rene Scott rehearses with Derrick Baskin (left) and Tyler Maynard. The actors wear outfits designed to help them anticipate the final costumes.

The ultimate ending to the power struggle between Ariel (Sierra Boggess) and Ursula (Sherie Rene Scott) was conceived between the Denver tryouts and the subsequent New York rehearsals.

a performer. That's what I think thrills an audience. You feel that they've invented it for you, and they're leaving a piece of their body on the stage for you to take home."

But to create these performances, and the "vehicles" (shows) in which the performances can thrive, involves refining a million infinitesimal details and asking question after question: what color should Prince Eric's jacket be? How many times should the set pieces unfurl and rotate and in what order? Is that the best key for this actor to sing in? Is the sound too brittle? A successful show is not just a product of a healthy collaboration among thoughtful artists, it's a culmination of countless decisions, and making the decisions involves eliminating the dross and trying to refine the jewels¬—and that process takes time, sometimes long, boring, chilly time.

This dreariest period, known as the technical rehearsals, is also, conversely, one of the most important. It's the polishing phase in the life of a gemstone that's already been cut. At tech rehearsals, every single lighting cue, music cue, sound cue, and stage cue is gone over many times and "set," which now in the theater includes being programmed into a computer. It's possible—even normal—to spend an entire eight- or ten-hour rehearsal period on eight or ten minutes of playing time. It can, and does, take weeks to get through the entire show.

During tech rehearsals actors have to time their quick changes; crosses behind or above or below the set have to be timed; dressers have to know where to be when; sometimes scenes have to be written to provide a few extra minutes for a change in scenery or clothes. The entire auditorium of the theater is full of work desks built above the seats. Each department has a desk and any number of computers. This is when all the fine details of the show are finalized for its final venue, the Broadway theater.

One of the most unsung heroes of a Broadway production is the sound designer. The sound designer is both a scientist of sorts—an expert in sound and how to make it, shape it, color, and amplify it—and an artist, creating something aesthetically pleasing that meshes with the rest of the show's spectacle and helps tell the script's story. Sound designer John Shivers has worked on a score of Broadway productions, including *Tarzan, Mary Poppins, The Lion King,* and *Elton John and Tim Rice's AIDA.* He's also worked for headliners Dionne Warwick, Gregory Hines, and Savion Glover.

Shivers talks about challenges rather than problems, but he had his share on *The Little Mermaid.* One of them is the theater itself and what he calls the "noise floor," which is, essentially, the amount of noise the theater and its equipment makes before an actor says a word or a musician plays a note. The Lunt-Fontanne, Shivers reports, has a very high noise floor. There is, for one, the air-conditioning system. Then there are the new powerful lighting instruments. "Each one of them makes a little noise," he says, "and when you put 150 of them together, they're making quite a bit of noise." Furthermore, the set has little to absorb the ambient sonic field.

The result? Mostly a loss of subtlety. And there are limits to how loud he can go: too much volume causes distortion. Shivers worries that some of the actual sound "underscoring" of the show—a meticulous and specific soundscape he created, as he does for each show, from his extensive library of sounds and other sources—isn't as crisp as it might be. He and lighting designer Natasha Katz worked together in

The Little Mermaid is the fifth Disney-on-Broadway gig for sound designer John Shivers.

keeping the noise at a manageable level. The video projectors were baffled, too, and a sound-dampening system was installed in the theater.

Shivers's soundscape included different basic sounds for each specific environment of the show: underwater, on land, in Ursula's lair. Those sounds, which he coordinated with Sven Ortel's animation scheme, needed to be loud enough to register on the ear, but couldn't mask the songs and dialogue. As for sound effects, Shivers subscribes to the notion that a sound effect must be accompanied by a visual cue. To Shivers, for example, not all bubbles are created equal. "You need to play around with them quite a bit. I mean, what would the bubbles sound like in Triton's court? What would be appropriate for Ursula's cave, given her role as a villain? They should sound eerie because that's the kind of character she is. Ariel has these tiny little cute bubble sounds associated with her grotto.

"A lot of what I do is lost on most people," Shivers says. "People don't usually sit in the audience thinking, 'Oh, good sound'—although they might notice if it's not good. Sometimes you don't hear it but it acts subconsciously. A lot of sound design communicates subliminally. I think that's the beauty of the design, that you can sway people, lead them into different moods or sets of emotions. That's the art of it, the storytelling part. I love that aspect of it."

"You can look at it . . . as the story for a girl who is going through what girls definitely go through, where they feel, 'I don't fit in my skin. I don't belong in this world. My whole being is changing. I want to go somewhere, be somewhere.'"
—FRANCESCA ZAMBELLO

BUT THERE WAS TO BE ONE more hurdle for *The Little Mermaid* to jump over, and it wasn't on the schedule.

On November 10 (the day scheduled for previews six and seven of *Mermaid*), Local One of the International Alliance of Theatrical Stage Employees (IATSE), the union representing Broadway's stagehands, called a strike. The actors' and musicians' unions refused to cross the stagehands' picket lines. Most of Broadway shut down. Times Square entered a weird state of suspended animation while everyone watched the perennially popular (and profitable) Thanksgiving weekend go by with most theaters empty. Disney cancelled *The Little Mermaid*'s December 6 opening and waited for the end of the negotiations.

The strike was settled on November 28, with closed shows resuming performances on November 29. Opening night for *The Little Mermaid* was rescheduled for 6:30 p.m. on Thursday, January 10, 2008.

The strike made the preview period for *Mermaid* even more delicate than usual. Some of the most important people in the life of this production had other commitments scheduled very soon after December. Francesca Zambello, for example, was to direct an opera at La Scala. She found herself commuting between rehearsals for *Cyrano de Bergerac* in Milan and *The Little Mermaid* at the Lunt-Fontanne on West 46th Street.

Sometimes, however, adversity works to a production's advantage, and there is no doubt that by the new opening night, the cast was psyched for success. They may not have had the unbroken performance momentum during previews the producers and creative contributors would have liked, but they were certainly ready to give opening night their all.

And so *The Little Mermaid* swam into the hearts of the Broadway audience. Ariel's voice was heard in a new production that proves how universal her story is. There is no question that the adults and children who fill the seats of the theater eight times a week enjoy the show. They make it known more than once during each performance just how pleased they are.

"This is a very important story to a lot of young women," says Francesca Zambello. "It's a universal story, written by a man. Still, there is a lot of special meaning for women, no matter how you look at it. You can look at it as a love story where the girl gets the guy, which is perhaps the more conventional. You can look at it, which I am more interested in, of course, as the story for

LEFT: Eric asks for Ariel's hand in marriage.
OPPOSITE: The wedding of Ariel and Eric, their happiness truly earned by them both.

a girl who is going through what girls definitely go through, where they feel, 'I don't fit in my skin. I don't belong in this world. My whole being is changing. I want to go somewhere, be somewhere.'

"I think every girl goes through that and can relate to that. You know, your body changes, and so forth. Then there is for me the really interesting thing that Ariel takes action: she goes to Ursula. At the end, it was important that we tell the story so that she resolves the plot. That she brings about the denouement. And so for me, those are all things that I think touch girls, I see it when I watch the show. I see it when I watch little girls watching it.

"Teenagers or girls in their early twenties are reliving what it meant to them as they were growing up and find it speaks to them even more now. And then the connection that is so special is the father-daughter connection. If you're your daddy's girl, and most girls are, that is a big thing. And watching fathers and daughters at the show together is almost more touching to me than watching mothers and daughters. I've seen it over and over where you just see these fathers weeping about someday losing their girl.

"When I see that kind of stuff, I get misty-eyed, but I also think we've made something that some people will remember forever. I mean, those kinds of experiences are seminal experiences that you do not forget. I think it's great that my job is to help make those emotions come to the surface."

And so the period of preparing *The Little Mermaid* for public view on Broadway came to an end. Not that the show is finished. For one thing, the producer still has changes up his sleeve for any future productions in the U.S. or abroad, or for domestic or foreign tours. Now that the story of Ariel has been given new life in a new medium, the question doesn't seem to be whether Ariel will be with us for a long time or not, but just where she will surface again to enchant us with her singular voice.

Opening Night: January 10, 2008
Lunt Fontanne Theatre

STAFF FOR *THE LITTLE MERMAID*

COMPANY MANAGER ....RANDY MEYER

Production Associate...............JANE ABRAMSON
Assistant Company Manager .... Margie Freeswick
Assistant to the Associate Producer ....
.... Kerry McGrath
Show Accountant............................ Barbara Toben

GENERAL PRESS REPRESENTATIVE
BONEAU/BRYAN-BROWN ....Chris Boneau
......................................Matt Polk, Adriana Douzos
.........................Juliana Hannett, Danielle Crinnion

Production Stage Manager ....Clifford Schwartz
Stage Manager ....Theresa Bailey
Assistant Stage Managers......... Kenneth J. McGee,
.... Matthew Aaron Stern, Sarah Tschirpke
Dance Captain............................ Joanne Manning
Assistant Dance Captain .... James Brown III
Fight Captain................................. James Brown III
Production Assistants .... Steven Malone
..............Jennifer Noterman, Thomas Recktenwald
.... Marielle Solan
Associate Scenic Designer .... Peter Eastman
Assistant Scenic Designer ....Denny Moyes
Scenic Design Assistants...............Gaetane Bertol
....................................Larry Brown, Kelly Hanson
.... Niki Hernandez-Adams, Nathan Heverin
.... Rachel Short Janocko, Jee an Jung, Mimi Lien
.................Frank McCullough, Arnulfo Maldonado
.............................Robert Pyzocha, Chisato Uno
Sculptor.......................................Arturs Virtmanis
Associate Costume Designer ...... Tracy Christensen
Assistant Costume Designers .... Brian J. Bustos
.... Amy Clark
Costume Shoppers......................Leon Dobkowski
....Vanessa Leuck
Associate Lighting Designer ....Yael Lubetzky
Lighting Design Assistant........ Craig Stelzenmuller
Automated Lighting Programmer ....
.... Aland Henderson
Automated Lighting Tracker...................Joel Shier
Assistant to the Lighting Designer..... Richard Swan
Associate Sound Designer ....David Patridge
Associate Hair Designer ....Jonathan Carter
Assistant Hair Designer ....Thomas Augustine
Projection Design Assistants............... Peter Acken
.... Katy Tucker
Associate Aerial Designer .... Angela Phillips

Magic/Illusion Designer ....Joe Eddie Fairchild
Associate to Technical Director ....Rose Palombo
Production Carpenter ....Stephen Detmer
Head Carpenter .... Patrick Eviston
Fly Automation .... Jeff Zink
Deck Automation.................Michael L. Shepp, Jr.
Rigger .... Rick Howard
Production Electrician........................ Rick Baxter
Head Electrician...........................Joseph Pearson
Assistant Electrician .... Damian Caza-Cleypool
Moving Light Technician ....Jesse Hancox
Production Props ....Jerry L. Marshall
Assistant Props .... Steven E. Wood
Production Sound Engineer............ David Patridge
Head Sound .... George Huckins
Deck Sound .... Scott Anderson
Wardrobe Supervisor................... Nancy Schaefer
Assistant Wardrobe Supervisor ... Edmund Harrison
Wardrobe Staff .... Vanessa Fernandez
.....................Kathleen Gallagher, Rachael Garrett
.... Sue Hamilton, Melanie Hansen
.... Amelia Haywood, Barbara Hladsky
.... Franklin Hollenbeck,Terry LaVada
........Robert J. MalkmusIII, Paul Riner, Eric Rudy
.... Rita Santi, Rodd Sovar
.................................Claire Verlaet, Jay Woods
Hair Supervisor ....Thomas Augustine
Assistant Hair Supervisor .... Gary Arave
Hairdressers .... Joshua First, Shanah Kendall
Make-Up Supervisor .... Tiffany Hicks
Assistant Make-Up Supervisor...........Jorge Vargas
Associate Music Director............... Greg Anthony
Additional Orchestrations.............. Larry Hochman
.... Michael Starobin
Music Preparation .... Anixter Rice Music Service
Electronic Music Design .... Andrew Barrett
...............................for Lionella Productions, Ltd.
Electronic Music Design Assistant........ Jeff Marder
Associate to Mr. Menken ....Rick Kunis
Rehearsal Drummer ....John Redsecker
Rehearsal Pianists...........................Aron Accurso
...................Matt Eisenstein, Andrew Grobengieser
Children's Vocal Coach...............Marianne Challis

ORCHESTRA

Conductor – Michael Kosarin
Associate Conductor – Greg Anthony
Electronic Music Design – Andrew Barrett

Concertmaster: Suzanne Ornstein; Violin:
Mineko Yajima; Cello 1: Roger Shell; Cello 2:

Deborah Assael-Migliore; Lead Trumpet: Nicholas
Marchione; Trumpet: Frank Greene;Trombone:
Gary Grimaldi; Bass Trombone/Tuba: Jeff Caswell;
Reed 1: Steve Kenyon; Reed 2: David Young; Reed
3: Marc Phanuef; French Horn: Zohar Schondorf;
Keyboard 1: Aron Accurso; Keyboard 2: Greg
Anthony; Keyboard 3: Andrew Grobengieser;
Bass: Richard Sarpola; Drums: John Redsecker;
Percussion: Joe Passaro

Music Coordinator : Michael Keller

TARA RUBIN CASTING
Tara Rubin, CSA, Eric Woodall, CSA, Laura
Schutzel, CSA, Merri Sugarman, CSA, Rebecca
Carfagna, Paige Blansfield, Dale Brown

AERIAL DESIGNER..............PICHÓN BALDINU

DIALOGUE & VOCAL COACH ....
....DEBORAH HECHT

Advertising............................Serino Coyne, Inc.
Press Associates .... Adrian Bryan-Brown
.... Aaron Meier, Christine Olver, Susanne Tighe
Logo Art ....Scott Thornley + Company
Production Photography ....Joan Marcus
Acoustic Consultant ..... Paul Scarbrough, A'Kustiks
Structural Engineering Consultant ....Bill Gorlin
.... McLaren, P.C.
Executive Travel ..... Robert Arnao, Patricia McRory
Production Travel............................ Jill L. Citron
Payroll Managers .... Anthony DeLuca
.... Cathy Guerra
Counsel – Immigration .... Michael Rosenfeld
Physical Therapy...
.......................The Green Room P.T./Heidi Green
Consulting Orthopedic Surgeon..........................
....Dr. Phillip Bauman
Chaperone ....John Mara
Children's Tutoring........... On Location Education/
.... Serena Stanley

CREDITS
Scenery by Showman Fabricators, Inc.; Show
Canada Industries; Adirondack Studios, Inc.; The
Paragon Innovation Group, Inc.; Proof Productions.
Automation of scenery and rigging by Showman
Fabricators, Inc., Long Island City, NY featur-
ing Raynok Motion Control. Lighting equipment
by PRG Lighting. Projection equipment by PRG

Lighting. Sound equipment by Sound Associates Inc. Costume construction by Parsons Meares Ltd.; Barbara Matera, Ltd.; Eric Winterling, Inc.; Tricorne, Inc.; Martin Izquierdo Studio. Custom millinery provided by Lynne Mackey Studio; Rodney Gordon; Arnold S. Levine, Inc.; Marian Jean Hose. Custom fabric dyeing and printing by Gene Mignola, Hochi Asiatico, Martin Izquierdo Studio, Olympus Flag and Banner. Costume painting by Hochi Asiatico, Virginia Clow, Claudia Dzundza, Martin Izquierdo Studio, Mary Macy, Parmelee Welles Tolkan, Margaret Peot. Custom footwear by Capri Shoes by Oscar Navarro; Handmade Shoes by Fred Longtin; LaDuca Shoes; Pluma Shoes by Walter Raimundo; Capezio. Custom jewelry and crafts by Arnold S. Levine, Inc.; Marian Jean Hose; Martin Izquierdo Studios; Gaetane Bertol; Larry Vrba. Undergarments by Bra*Tenders; On Stage Dancewear. Ursula mechanics by Jon Gellman Effects. Mermaid tails by Michael Curry Design, Inc. Eel electrics by Birtek Specialty Lighting. Knitwear provided by Karen Eifert and Maria Ficalora Knitwear, Ltd. Wigs by Bob Kelly Wigs; Ray Marston Wigs; Victoria Wood. Props by Arnold S. Levine, Inc.; Jerard Studio; Michael Curry Design, Inc.; The Paragon Innovation Group, Inc.; Provost Displays; I.C.B.A; Puppet Heap; Rabbit's Choice; Vogue Too; Zoë Morsette. Ricola natural herb cough drops courtesy of Ricola USA, Inc. Emergen-C health and energy drink mix provided by Alacer Corp.

Make Up Provided By M•A•C.

Gliding By Heelys®.

THE LITTLE MERMAID originally premiered at the Ellie Caulkins Opera House, Denver Center for the Performing Arts, Colorado.

THE LITTLE MERMAID rehearsed at the New 42nd Street Studios.

SPECIAL THANKS
James M. Nederlander, James L. Nederlander, Nick Scandalios, Herschel Waxman, Jim Boese of the Nederlander Organization, Kate Boucher, Ian Galloway and Dan Murtha of Bolt Action Five, Michael Curry, Jackie Galloway, HelenGoddard, Michael Harrell of MHNY Wardrobe Services, Inc., Green Hippo, Nichol Hignite, Courtney Hoffman, Diana Kuriyama, Anna Ledwich, Roland Wolfe of Saks Fifth Avenue and the styling team at the Fifth Avenue Club, Larry Sonn, Georgia Stitt, Crystal Thompson, Walt Disney Imagineering R&D.

DISNEY THEATRICAL PRODUCTIONS

President ....Thomas Schumacher
EVP & Managing Director ....David Schrader
SVP & General Manager ....Alan Levey
SVP, Creative Affairs....................Michele Steckler
SVP, International...............................Ron Kollen
Vice President, Operations ....Dana Amendola
Vice President, Labor Relations ....Allan Frost
Vice President, Worldwide Publicity
    & Communications......................Joe Quenqua
Vice President, Domestic Touring .... Jack Eldon
Vice President, Theatrical Licensing ....
....Steve Fickinger
Vice President, Human Resources ......June Heindel
Director, Domestic Touring ....Michael Buchanan
Director, Casting & Development ....
....Jennifer Rudin, CSA
Manager, Labor Relations............Stephanie Cheek
Manager, Human Resources ....Jewel Neal
Manager, Information Systems ....Scott Benedict
Senior Computer Support Analyst......................
....Kevin A. McGuire
Senior IT Support Analyst...................Andy Singh
IT/Business Analyst ....William Boudiette

Production
Executive Music Producer ....Chris Montan
Vice President, Physical Production ....
....John Tiggeloven
Senior Manager, International ....Michael Cassel
Senior Manager, Safety ....Canara Price
Manager, Physical Production ......Karl Chmielewski
Staff Associate Designer ....Dennis W. Moyes
Dramaturg & Literary Manager .... Ken Cerniglia

Marketing
Vice President, Broadway..................Andrew Flatt
Vice President, International............Fiona Thomas
Director, Broadway............................Kyle Young
Director, Education & Outreach..........Peter Avery
Senior Manager, Broadway ....Michele Groner
Website Manager ....Eric W. Kratzer
Media Asset Manager...................Cara L. Moccia
Assistant Manager, Communications ...Dana Torres
Assistant Manager, Promotions ....Craig Buckley

Sales
Director, National Sales ....Bryan Dockett
Manager, New Business Development ....
....Jacob Lloyd Kimbro
Manager, Sales & Ticketing................ Nick Falzon
Manager, Group Sales .... Juil Kim

Business and Legal Affairs
Senior Vice President ....Jonathan Olson
Vice President ....Robbin Kelley
Executive Director........................Harry S. Gold
Senior Counsel ....Seth Stuhl
Paralegal/Contract Administration ....Colleen Lober

Finance
Director ....Joe McClafferty
Senior Manager, Finance...................Dana James
Manager, Finance ....John Fajardo
Manager, Production Accounting ....Liza Breslin
Production Accountants......................Joy Brown
...................................Nick Judge, Barbara Toben
Assistant Production Accountant ......Isander Rojas
Senior Financial Analyst ....Tatiana Bautista
Senior Sales Analyst ....Liz Jurist Schwarzwalder

Administrative Staff
Dusty Bennett, Amy Caldamone, Lauren Daghini, Surayah Davis, Jessica Doina, Cristi Finn, Cristina Fowler, Dayle Gruet, Gregory Hanoian, Jonathan Hanson, Jay Hollenback, Connie Jasper, Tom Kingsley, Kerry McGrath, Lisa Mitchell, Melanie Montes, Ryan Pears, Jessica Powers, Roberta Risafi, Colleen Rosati, Kisha Santiago, David Scott, Benjy Shaw, Kyle Wilson, Jason Zammit

DISNEY THEATRICAL MERCHANDISE
Vice President ....Steven Downing
Operations Manager.......................Shawn Baker
Merchandise Manager ....Neil Markman
Associate Buyer ....Violet Burlaza
Assistant Manager, Inventory...........Suzanne Jakel
Retail Supervisor...................Michael Giammatteo
On-Site Retail Manager ....Jeff Knizner
On-Site Assistant Retail Manager ....Mark Murynec

Disney Theatrical Productions
c/o The New Amsterdam Theatre
214 West 42nd Street
New York, NY 10036
www.disneyonbroadway.com

Fin

ACKNOWLEDGMENTS

The publisher and producer would like to thank the many individuals who helped to make this book possible:
Jane Abramson, Dusty Bennett, Karl Chmielewski, Tracy Christensen, Lauren Daghini, Michael Dei Cas,
Steven Downing, Peter Eastman, Amanda Jones, Jeff Kurtti, Todd Lacy, Kerry McGrath, Randy Meyer, Lisa Mitchell,
Cara Moccia, Andrea Recendez, Sven Ortel, Thomas Schumacher, Ed Squair, George Tsypin, Kyle Young,
and our friends at Disney's Animation Research Library (Fox Carney, Doug Engalla, Ann Hansen, Lella Smith,
Jackie Vasquez, and Mary Walsh).

For information address Disney Editions, 114 Fifth Avenue, New York, New York 10011-5690.
Editorial Director: Wendy Lefkon
Senior Editor: Jody Revenson
Assistant Editor: Jessica Ward

Academy Award® and Oscar® are registered trademarks of the Academy of Motion Picture Arts and Sciences.
Tony® is a registered trademark of the American Theater Wing.
Grammy® is a registered trademark of the National Academy of Recording Arts and Sciences, Inc.
Golden Globe(s)® is a registered trademark of the Academy of Television Arts and Sciences/National Television Academy.

Except as noted below, all photographs of the production and rehearsal of
The Little Mermaid, A Broadway Musical, were taken by Joan Marcus
Page 22: Tony Craddock/Stone/Getty Images
Page 23: The Bridgeman Art Library/Getty Images
Page 24: (bottom left) Anne Grahame Johnstone/The Bridgeman Art Library/Getty Images;
(top right) © Cynthia Hart Designer/Corbis
Pages 34, 59 (top right), and 61 (center): Per Breiehagen
Pages 120 (bottom left, center, and middle right) and 121: Randy Meyer

"Daughters of Triton," "Part of Your World," "Under the Sea," "Poor Unfortunate Souls," "Les Poissons," "Kiss the Girl"
Lyrics by Howard Ashman
© 1988 Walt Disney Music Company (ASCAP)
All rights reserved. Lyrics reprinted by permission.

"Fathoms Below," "Finale"
Lyrics by Howard Ashman and Glenn Slater
© 2007 Walt Disney Music Company (ASCAP) Punchbuggy Music (ASCAP)
All rights reserved. Lyrics reprinted by permission.

"The World Above," "Human Stuff," "I Want the Good Times Back," "She's in Love," "Her Voice," "Sweet Child,"
"Positoovity," "Beyond My Wildest Dreams," "One Step Closer," "The Contest"
Lyrics by Glenn Slater
© 2007 Walt Disney Music Company (ASCAP) / Punchbuggy Music (ASCA))
All rights reserved. Lyrics reprinted by permission.

Library of Congress Cataloging-in-Publication Data on file
ISBN 978-1-4231-1272-3

Produced by Welcome Enterprises, Inc.
6 West 18th Street, New York, New York 10011
www.welcomebooks.com
Project Director: H. Clark Wakabayashi
A Greg/Clark Design

Printed in China
FIRST EDITION
1 3 5 7 9 10 8 6 4 2